"They're getting nervous and that makes you a target."

"Makes us both targets," she amended.

He nodded. "They don't like that we're getting so close."

Close. Yes. Too close. This close she could see the tiny gray specks that gave his deep blue eyes such depth and vividness. She liked his lips… the cut of his jaw and the impact of his high cheekbones. The blue eyes appeared even more profound framed by that coal-black hair.

"You keep looking at me that way and we're going to have a problem."

"What kind of problem?" she prompted. Did she have to spell it out?

"The kind where I end that long dry spell of no kisses."

She moistened her lips. "I wouldn't categorize that as a problem."

He leaned closer. "In that case—" he brushed his lips against hers "—let's bring on the rain."

DEBRA WEBB

COLBY VELOCITY

TORONTO • NEW YORK • LONDON
AMSTERDAM • PARIS • SYDNEY • HAMBURG
STOCKHOLM • ATHENS • TOKYO • MILAN • MADRID
PRAGUE • WARSAW • BUDAPEST • AUCKLAND

This book is dedicated to my two dearest friends,
Vicki Hinze and Peggy Webb.
Two of the most amazing ladies
I have ever had the privilege
to know and love!

ISBN-13: 978-0-373-74543-2

COLBY VELOCITY

This edition published by arrangement with Harlequin Books S.A.

For questions and comments about the quality of this book please contact us at Customer_eCare@Harlequin.ca.

www.eHarlequin.com

Printed in U.S.A.

ABOUT THE AUTHOR

Debra Webb wrote her first story at age nine and her first romance at thirteen. It wasn't until she spent three years working for the military behind the Iron Curtain and within the confining political walls of Berlin, Germany, that she realized her true calling. A five-year stint with NASA on the Space Shuttle Program reinforced her love of the endless possibilities within her grasp as a storyteller. A collision course between suspense and romance was set. Debra has been writing romantic suspense and action-packed romantic thrillers since. Visit her at www.DebraWebb.com or write to her at P.O. Box 4889, Huntsville, AL 35815.

Books by Debra Webb

HARLEQUIN INTRIGUE

1023—COLBY REBUILT*
1042—GUARDIAN ANGEL*
1071—IDENTITY UNKNOWN*
1092—MOTIVE: SECRET BABY
1108—SECRETS IN FOUR CORNERS
1145—SMALL-TOWN SECRETS††
1151—THE BRIDE'S SECRETS††
1157—HIS SECRET LIFE††
1173—FIRST NIGHT*
1188—COLBY LOCKDOWN**
1194—COLBY JUSTICE**
1216—COLBY CONTROL§
1222—COLBY VELOCITY§

*Colby Agency
††Colby Agency: Elite Reconnaissance Division
**Colby Agency: Under Siege
§Colby Agency: Merger

CAST OF CHARACTERS

Leland "Rocky" Rockford—A former Equalizer, Rocky has an aversion to suits. But if you're going through a door to face the unknown, he's the man you want at your side.

Kendra Todd—Kendra is conservative and sophisticated. She loves her work at the Colby Agency. Returning to her old life wasn't on her agenda until an old friend calls.

Yoni Sayar—A rising star in D.C.'s political world...he is desperate for Kendra's help.

Judd Castille—He's a U.S. senator whose power may or may not have turned him to the dark side.

Wayne Burton—Homicide detective Burton seems to want to help Kendra...she once shared his bed, after all.

Aleesha Ferguson—Just another dead prostitute...or is she more?

Sharon Castille—The senator's wife. What is she running from?

Grant Roper—Senator Castille's new personal aide. How far is he willing to go to move up the ranks?

Patsy Talley and Levi Stark—Members of the Colby Agency research staff.

Victoria Colby-Camp—As the head of the Colby Agency Victoria is committed to making the merger between her agency and the Equalizers work.

Jim Colby—Jim wants his mother to be happy, no matter what it takes. He now helps her run the Colby Agency.

Ian Michaels—As Victoria's second-in-command, Ian is a stabilizing force as the Colby Agency staff and the former Equalizers merge.

Chapter One

Chicago, Tuesday, July 4, 9:00 p.m.

Kendra Todd surveyed the deserted street. The last of the lingering Fourth of July revelers were only a few blocks over. The fireworks at the Pier crackled in the air, sending sprays of light over the city.

She had attended the agency cookout at Jim Colby's home. Afterward she'd anticipated a quiet evening at her apartment… but that hadn't happened.

Talk about ghosts from the past…. The frantic call she'd received had taken her back several years. Three, to be exact.

To a place she'd just as soon not revisited.

9:04 p.m. He was late.

Kendra tucked her cell phone back into the holster on her belt and surveyed the street once more.

Ten minutes more of hanging around this street corner alone and she was out of here. Whatever her old friend's latest drama…it wasn't hers. Kendra Todd was no longer a part of the D.C. world of ruthless ambition and colliding egos. In three years she hadn't looked back once.

The move to Chicago was the smartest choice she'd made in a very long time. Working with Chicago PD's community affairs division the first two years of her new Windy City life had been very useful in acquainting herself with this new environment. Last year's offer to join the staff of the Colby Agency had come after working closely with Ian Michaels during the abduction attempt of Victoria Colby-Camp's granddaughter. The opportunity had proven the perfect prompt for Kendra to make a major move toward personally recognizing and professionally achieving a true career goal.

Reaching out to those in need and using the interactive skills she'd honed so well to solve a case satisfied her in a way nothing else about her professional history had. The camaraderie at the Colby Agency surprised her still. For someone who had no family left and who'd walked away from her lifelong friends three years ago, the atmosphere at the agency was spot on. She not only liked her job as an investigator, she also liked being part of something real.

Real life. Real people.

To say this jolt from the past was unwelcome would be a vast understatement. Not that she hadn't kept in touch with a few of her former associates. Christmas cards and the occasional birthday card were exchanged. At first she'd even exchanged e-mails with her former boyfriend, but that had fizzled out after only a few months. But this—tonight—was far from a mere unexpected call from an old colleague.

This was trouble in big, bold letters.

Headlights flashed, drawing her attention to the west end of the block. A dark nondescript sedan had made the turn at the intersection and now rolled slowly in her direction.

She maintained her position against the wall of the closed boutique and watched as the sedan pulled up to the curb directly behind her smaller, two-door sports car. The snazzy red car was her one visible capitulation to vanity. And maybe to independence from all the *red* tape and chaos of so-called organized government.

The driver's door opened and she held her breath. As soon as the head and torso rose from behind the wheel of the car she squinted to identify the driver. The street lamp's glow spread across the hood of the sedan but fell short of providing sufficient illumination beyond the windshield. But she would know that tall, slim frame anywhere…even in the dark.

Yoni Sayar straightened his suit jacket and shoved the car door closed.

Kendra couldn't deny some sense of sentimentality at seeing him. Three years was a long time and they had been good friends.

"Kendra." He smiled as he strode toward her.

"It's good to see you," she confessed before accepting his quick, firm embrace.

Tall, thin and dark, Yoni was a natural born American but his parents were Israeli immigrants. Both had worked hard to ensure he received the best education possible and were extraordinarily proud of his accomplishments. A master's degree in global communications was complemented by his ability to speak a number of languages with incredible ease and fluency. He'd turned down numerous lucrative corporate offers to pursue his goal of making a difference in the merciless world of politics. A lobbyist who supported the rights of main street Americans over those of corporate America.

Yoni was one of the good guys. He'd worked hard to earn the respect of the most powerful senators and congressional members, including Senator Judd Castille, Kendra's former boss.

After a thorough scrutiny of her face, he said, "You look very happy." He nodded his approval. "Happy and stress-free."

A moment's hesitation passed before she admitted, "I'm very happy." Old habits died hard. Even with a good friend like Yoni, the political arena had made her wary of the slightest personal confession. "The Colby Agency is great. It's the best move I could have made."

He surveyed the deserted street. "I'm very pleased to hear this." His tone gave away his distraction more so than his not so discreet surveillance of their surroundings.

"Would you like to have coffee while we talk?" He'd insisted on meeting someplace where they wouldn't be seen. Another learned trait of the political life. Still, surely he didn't expect to talk right here on the street, deserted or not. He'd come all this way, the least she could do was buy him a cup of coffee.

He shook his head. "I can't risk being seen."

With you. That he didn't verbalize that part disturbed her on some level. She and Senator Castille had parted on less than favorable terms. That was no secret. The rumors that had at first buzzed in the media were quickly squashed by Castille's people. It was completely understandable that Yoni would not want to be spied collaborating with the enemy.

Even three years later she remained the enemy.

"All right." She gestured to her car. "Why don't we sit in my car?"

He glanced nervously at the vehicle parked in front of his rental. "Well...we can do that."

That his uneasiness continued to mount triggered the first, distant alarm. Kendra led the way, hitting the remote and unlocking the doors as they reached the vehicle. She settled behind the steering wheel and waited until he'd slid into the passenger seat next to her before locking the doors once more.

"You bought a new car." He looked around the interior, surprise in his expression. "It's very nice." He managed a lackluster smile. "It suits you."

"It was time." The interior lights dimmed automatically, leaving them in darkness.

It was his turn to speak. This was his rendezvous after all. Yet the silence dragged on several seconds adding to Kendra's uneasiness. "Why don't you start at the beginning?" No point beating around the bush. He'd asked for this meeting, had taken a flight, rented a car and met her in an out-of-the-way location. A scene right out of an espionage movie.

Yoni released a big breath. "You know how Castille is. If he smells trouble..."

Trouble. There it was. She'd known it was coming. "I thought you and Castille were still tight." The truth was, when Castille had targeted her, Yoni hadn't gone out of his way to back her up. She'd understood at the time, still did actually. Once Castille had decided she was out, no one or nothing was going to change his mind. Yoni sticking his neck out and damaging his own position with the arrogant senator wouldn't have helped Kendra.

Political life was ruthless.

A frown furrowed across her brow as all those frustrating memories tumbled into vivid recollection. How the heck had she allowed herself to be dragged back into this vicious cycle?

"What sort of trouble?" And what did it have to do with her? Kendra tamped down the frustration. She reminded herself that she'd heard something in his voice that concerned her when he'd called. She couldn't just ignore him if he really needed help.

"I'm certain you've heard about the Transparency Bill."

She'd heard. Anyone who read the newspaper or watched the news likely knew of it. The bill was a very progressive action that had raised lots of eyebrows, particularly on Capitol Hill. Ultimately if the bill was passed, the way lobbyists and special interests groups worked would be forever changed. For the better. Though those lobbyists and special interest groups didn't see it that way.

"Castille supports it," she acknowledged. That she knew based on the headlines. "He's taken a lot of heat from the groups he once allowed to bolster his nest egg." Oh, yes. Castille was one rich old man. He'd reveled in the fringe benefits of those who lobbied for his support. Now that he was nearing retirement he'd opted to man-up and do what no other senator before him had had the courage to do. Limit the behind-the-scenes influence and reach of all those very groups who fueled the power.

"He has persuaded a number to follow suit," Yoni mentioned, not that it was necessary. Kendra knew very well how much influence Castille wielded.

She turned to her old friend, searched his face. Her eyes had grown accustomed to the low light. "I can see where you might not be a supporter of the proposed legislation."

He shook his head. "I helped design the bill."

"Are you serious?" It was difficult to imagine Yoni, a lobbyist, proposing anything that would limit his ability to do his job. Though his efforts were always forthright and just, there were necessary strategies that those outside the political playing field might not fully understand if those efforts were exposed. Serving the greater good came with a cost—usually associated with providing benefits for certain private groups. It was simply the way the world worked.

Yoni dropped his head back against the seat and released a weary breath. "The whole process has gotten out of control. Someone has to draw a line somewhere. I admire Castille for having the courage to do so."

No question about the need for stronger boundaries. She'd thought as much three years ago. That was just one of the subjects about which she and Castille had butted heads.

"I can see where that move would make you more than a few enemies." Was that why he'd come to her? Didn't make a whole lot of sense considering she was many degrees removed, but he hadn't actually given her any real specifics yet.

"Frustration, anger, resentment—all those things I anticipated," he explained, "but not the hideous threat of blackmail."

"Blackmail?" Her confusion cleared. "Someone is attempting to blackmail you?"

He nodded. "I have until ten Friday morning to ensure the senator ushers through a couple of amendment attachments or, according to the note I received, I'll face the consequences."

Tension tightened her muscles. "Do you have the note with you?"

He reached inside his summer-weight jacket and pulled out an envelope.

Kendra tapped a button to illuminate a console light. She accepted the envelope and inspected the exterior. His name was carefully printed on the front and nothing more. "Where was it delivered?"

"To my office. It was pushed beneath the door before we opened. I found it this morning."

Which meant anyone could have delivered it. Yoni's office was in downtown D.C. on a public block with little or no security measures. She opened the envelope and withdrew the single page typed note.

You know what you need to do. Friday, 10:00 a.m.is the deadline. Meet the demand or face the consequences.

"Have you been to the police?" The answer would be no, otherwise they wouldn't be sitting here going through the cloak-and-dagger motions.

"I can't go to the police."

"Why not?" That made no sense. "This threat could be more than an opportunistic scare tactic. You need to take it seriously." He'd been in this business long enough to know this already. Power and money were strong motivators; some would do anything to get their hands on one or both.

"There's another note."

That he didn't make eye contact was more telling than he realized. She'd understood there surely was one or more other notes since this one did not state the precise demands or consequences. "Did you bring that note, as well?" Was he really going to make her ask for every iota of information?

He retrieved another plain white envelope from his interior jacket pocket and handed it to her. When her fingers tightened on the envelope, he hesitated before letting go. "I don't want this ugliness to color your opinion of me." The worry in his eyes backed up the voiced concern.

"You know me better than that." She pulled the envelope free of his hold.

Yoni's name on the front. Inside, the letter was typed just like the other one, except this one was actually a copy of a press statement dated for Friday. The statement explained how a highly respected D.C. lobbyist had more than his share of skeletons in his closet. Kendra felt her jaw drop as she read the accusations that ran the gamut from illicit sexual behavior to fraternizing with known terrorists.

She carefully folded the letter, tucked it into the envelope once more and passed it back to him. "First, I need to know one thing."

"Anything."

'How many of those accusations are true even in the remotest sense?"

"You can't be serious."

The barely restrained inflection of outrage in his tone was without doubt authentic. She knew him well enough to know it when she heard it. Despite how strongly she felt about him as a person, she also fully understood that no one ever knew anyone *completely*. "Not a single word of it?" she pressed.

He moved his head side to side solemnly but firmly. "Not one word."

"I take it you want me to find out who's behind this threat."

Another of those weary sighs escaped his lips. "I didn't want to drag you into this, Kendra. But I'm desperate. There can be no evidence of these accusations because they are irrefutably false. But you know what a scandal like this could do to my reputation. False or not, I would be ruined on too many levels. Not to mention it could serve to undo much of what I've worked so hard to accomplish. I believe it is related to the bill Senator Castille and I are pushing. The bill is far too important to allow extortion to stop it. Can you and this Colby Agency you love so much help me?"

Kendra didn't allow herself the time to think about how she had sworn she would never go back to D.C. This was the trouble she had fully expected when the call had come. Yet, this was Yoni, her friend. A genuine hero of the people.

She couldn't turn her back on him.

"You understand that this will require your complete cooperation?"

"Yes, yes. Whatever you need."

"And we may have to bring the senator into it."

"Whatever we have to do," he reiterated.

"All right. I can help you," she said,

determined to make it so, no matter that the voice of reason shouted at her that it was indisputably a mistake. "More important, the Colby Agency can help you."

Chapter Two

Chicago, Wednesday, 5:00 a.m.

The vibration of metal on wood jarred Leland Rockford from a dead sleep. He rolled over and plopped a hand on the table next to his bed. His eyes refused to open as he fumbled across the table top for his cell phone. It shimmied in his hand as he grasped it.

With a flick of his thumb he slid the nuisance open. His eyelids reluctantly raised and he stared at the digital numbers on the alarm clock. 5:01 a.m. Who would call him at such an ungodly hour?

"Rockford," he mumbled, then cleared his throat.

"Rocky, it's Jim. We need you here ASAP."

His boss. Jim Colby's tone was clipped, tense. Not good. After last week's false labor alarm, his boss was seriously on edge. Rocky threw the sheet back and sat up, dropping his feet to the carpeted floor. "What's up?"

"I'm sending you on assignment in D.C. Come prepared to leave immediately."

Rocky scrubbed a hand through his sleep-tousled hair. "On my way."

He closed the phone and dropped it back onto the table. Okay. D.C. That meant he had to pack a suit. He hated suits. Hated dealing with rich hotshots who thought they owned the world.

Exhaling a blast of frustration, he pushed up from the bed. First a quick shower and a cup of coffee to boost his sluggish brain.

"You getting up?"

Damn. He'd forgotten that he had a guest. "Gotta go out of town for work."

The lamp on the right side of the bed switched on, highlighting the blond tresses spread across the pillow next to his. "Now?" she asked, squinting at the light.

"Now. I'll call you when I get back." He didn't wait for additional questions. Time was limited. Jim would be waiting for him.

Hurrying through a hot shower, he dried his hair with the towel then wrapped it around his waist and hesitated before stepping out of the bathroom and into his bedroom. When he did he experienced a distinct sense of relief that his guest hadn't hung around to chat. She'd left a note on his pillow.

I'll be waiting....

Rocky couldn't help feeling a little guilty. She was a nice lady. They'd gone out several times over the past couple of months and he liked her. But he just couldn't see the attraction between them as anything beyond basic lust. To be fair he'd tried. More for her sake than his own. She deserved his respect and at least a half-hearted attempt. Maybe when he returned from D.C. they would have that uncomfortable it's-not-working talk he'd been putting off.

These days he wasn't into pursuing dead ends. Or lust...just for the sake of a good time.

Not that he didn't like bachelorhood or hadn't enjoyed his share of no-strings-attached relationships, but at thirty-five it was getting a bit old. Time to think about a permanent relationship. Maybe even kids. His parents would love that.

That thought kicked his brain into gear.

Had he just used that particular four-letter word?

Kids.

Guys didn't have biological clocks, he was relatively certain, but it sure as hell felt like he could hear one ticking inordinately loudly in some mutinous region of his brain.

He hesitated as he pulled on a pair of jeans. A part of him wanted to deny the concept, but he wasn't into denial, either. Came with the territory when a guy was raised by parents who were practicing psychologists. Denial of one's feelings equated to fear. Suck up some courage and face the facts.

It was time to settle down and do the family thing.

All he had to do was find the right woman. He'd bought the house with the big yard. His finances were in order. Seemed as good a time as any.

All he needed was a good woman who respected his idiosyncrasies and his work. He had plenty of the former, like being a slob around the house. Watching sports and shouting at the refs on the television screen. Preparing gourmet meals. Something he and his father had in common. His entire life Rocky had remained convinced that his father the shrink was in fact a closet chef.

Rocky didn't want anybody in his kitchen. And his work was his top priority. Finding a woman who didn't mind relinquishing control in the kitchen likely wouldn't be a problem. Finding one who could live with him gone for days on end more often than not was another matter altogether. That was going to be the tough hurdle.

He grabbed a shirt from the top of the stack on the chair next to his closet, which was generally about as close to the closet as his laundry made it.

He wasn't worried about finding the right woman. One of these days when he least expected it, he would stumble on the one for him.

He glanced at the note on his pillow. But he wasn't going to hold his breath.

Colby Agency, 7:05 a.m.

"SINCE YONI SAYAR," Jim Colby explained as the briefing in Victoria Colby-Camp's office came to a conclusion, "was murdered outside his Crystal City apartment at three o'clock this morning—not even four hours ago—there's no word from the police as to the suspected motive. If they know anything, which is doubtful, they're not telling. I've asked the liaison to keep us informed but there are no guarantees. This is a politically sensitive situation and

I don't expect to be kept in the loop beyond what the rest of the world will see and hear in the media."

Rocky divided his attention between his boss and Victoria, the head of the Colby Agency. Despite this year's merger, Rocky couldn't help considering himself and the other Equalizers, including Jim, as separate from the rest of the Colby staff. The transition had moved along smoothly for the most part so far. He supposed it would simply take time to feel as if he "fit in" here the way he had in the old brownstone a world away from this ritzy location.

Victoria gestured to Kendra Todd, the Colby investigator who sat on the same side of the small conference table as Rocky and with whom he would be working on this assignment. "Kendra, do you have anything else to add?"

Kendra had explained Sayar's position in D.C. politics and his unexpected meeting with her less than twelve hours ago. She remained clearly shaken by the news of his murder. That fact had not stopped her from plunging into a strategy for determining the truth about this tragic event. She'd spoken with Sayar's parents an hour ago to pass along her reassurances that she would personally see that the investigation was conducted without bias and in a speedy manner.

"Nothing more as of yet," Kendra began, her voice weary. "I want you and Jim" she glanced from her boss to Rocky's "to know how much I appreciate the agency's support in this…investigation."

Typically the agency—as had been the case with the Equalizers—had at least one client who was very much alive before delving into a case. This situation was a little outside the norm since the client was now dead, but both Victoria and Jim felt strongly about finding the truth, particularly since Sayar had come to Kendra just before his murder.

"You have our full support," Victoria reiterated. "The Colby jet is standing by. Whatever resources you need on this end will be available."

"Going in blind like this," Jim took up where his mother left off, "and with the murder of Mr. Sayar, we believe it wise to be fully prepared. With that in mind, we're recommending you both carry your weapons. D.C.'s new handgun regulations are somewhat more relaxed, so there's no worry on that count."

Carrying personal protection was standard operation procedure for Equalizer cases, but the Colby Agency saw things differently. No weapons unless absolutely necessary. Rocky felt a sense of relief at this news. He much preferred being armed.

"Thank you." Kendra stood. "I'm ready," she looked expectantly at Rocky, "if you're all set."

Rocky pushed to his feet. "I'm good to go." He didn't have to ask who would be serving as lead on the case. For now, the Colby investigator assigned was in charge. That was fine by him. He had a reputation for being a rogue when it came to strategy in the field, and though he liked to bend the rules he rarely broke those rules. Not his style.

Within ten minutes they had picked up their weapons and bags, loaded into the agency car and headed for the airfield. Since Kendra didn't appear to be interested in conversation, Rocky passed the travel time reviewing Sayar's dossier a second time. Mostly he needed a distraction to keep his mind off how good she smelled. The scent was soft, subtle and sweet. Womanly.

But he was ignoring that.

She was friendly enough in a very professional way, but she paid little or no attention to him on any other level. Why should she? They were colleagues, nothing more. Obviously he wasn't her type.

He reread the last paragraph he'd perused. Sayar had no criminal record, not even a parking ticket. Top of his class at Vanderbilt University. Hardworking family. No ticked off ex-girlfriends. According to his family, Sayar never complained about work or any of his professional associates. This tragedy was a complete shock to all who knew him, again, according to the family. The tragedy was too fresh. Later when the shock wore off a little, one or both parents might remember little seemingly insignificant details they couldn't recall now.

Rocky closed the file and slid it into his bag. Whatever the victim's family thought or recalled, something was going on. Otherwise Sayar wouldn't have come to Kendra. Problem was, he was dead and all Rocky and Kendra had were questions.

Kendra stared out the car window at the passing cityscape. Rocky took advantage of her preoccupation to study his partner for this assignment. She was young, twenty-eight compared to his thirty-five. Long hair, more blond than brown. Smooth skin that seemed to be perpetually tanned. High cheekbones, thin nose and extra full lips. Big, brown eyes that reflected utter brilliance and deep compassion. Always conservatively dressed, but those modest skirts did nothing to disguise her tall, slender, well-toned frame. During the siege of the agency back in January he'd caught himself staring at her more than once. A very attractive woman.

But what he liked about her most was her extraordinarily ladylike manners. She reminded him of his mother. Prim, proper—classy—and always going out of her way to be helpful. He'd asked around about her social life and he'd learned a sad truth. Kendra Todd was all work and no play. She rarely dated. Never looked at him as anything other than a fellow investigator. Never looked at any of the males around the office in an unbusinesslike manner.

He'd asked her to lunch once but she'd declined, opting to remain at her desk with a sandwich from home. She was the first woman he'd been attracted to who wasn't attracted to him first.

Strange.

Even stranger, he was attracted to her and she wasn't actually his type. Kendra Todd possessed all those traits that he respected in his mother, but she was way too focused on business at this stage in her life.

Way too uptight for him.

She turned in his direction, her questioning gaze colliding with his.

Rocky blinked. Busted. "Sorry about your friend." Shaky recovery but at least he'd gotten out something rational.

"Thank you." She smoothed a hand over her cream-colored skirt and cleared her throat, simultaneously shifting her gaze forward.

The awkward silence that followed squeezed the air right out of the car.

Only one way to alleviate the tension. "You had time to lay out a preliminary strategy?" Safe enough question, he supposed.

A moment passed while she chewed her bottom lip. "I'm going straight to the top."

He lifted his eyebrows in question. "Senator Castille?"

"Yes."

Could prove dicey. "You think he'll see you?" At the briefing she'd mentioned that her parting with the senator had been less than pleasant.

"No."

"I guess you have a plan B." Rocky knew enough about her to fully understand that she wouldn't take no for an answer without a fight.

Kendra turned her attention back to him. "He will see me. He won't like it. He'll evade my attempts, ignore my questions, but he *will* eventually admit defeat."

Approval tugged at one corner of Rocky's mouth. Oh yeah, this lady was a ferocious tiger despite her sweet little kitten appearance. Something else he appreciated about her. "So you're fairly certain the senator is involved somchow."

"I'm certain of nothing," she pointed out. "I feel confident that he is well aware of whatever rumors are traveling the grapevine regarding the murder. Those rumors might provide leads."

"What about other lobbyists? Personal friends?" Judging by the stack of notes she had in that briefcase of hers, she'd done some serious research in the hours after her meeting with Sayar. Rocky doubted she'd gotten much sleep.

"There are two close associates, Stanford Smith and Ella Hendrix, who have publicly slammed his support of a controversial bill." Kendra took a deep breath and appeared to consider her next words before continuing. "It would be too easy, not to mention stupid," she glanced knowingly at Rocky, "for either one of them to be the one we're looking for. But, like the senator, they will be privy to rumors, incidents, that we need to know that might propel our investigation in the proper direction."

Rocky hadn't thought of it until now but he wondered if a lack of a real social life was a lingering side effect of D.C. politics. According to the dossier, Sayar had no notable social life. Rocky opted to ask about that later. To ask now might back up any suspicions she had about catching him staring at her. Every time he had the opportunity to study her he noticed something new.

Like the small sprinkling of freckles across her nose. He'd never noticed that before. Then again, he'd never sat this close to her in a confined space for this length of time. When she smiled, those extra full lips revealed gleaming white teeth that were far from perfectly straight. Just a little crooked. Just enough to give her smile special character.

He liked that about her. Gorgeous but not too perfect.

He seemed to like a lot of things about her.

"Did you have suggestions on where to begin?"

It wasn't until she asked the question that he realized she was openly watching him stare at her. He swallowed. Told himself to say something. "We should, of course, check out his residence. Often when someone feels cornered or afraid, he or she will hide information in a safe place in hopes of keeping a secret." He didn't look away when he ran out of logical suggestions. No point pretending he hadn't been staring. She'd caught him red-handed. Twice now.

"We'll go there tonight when the police have finished their investigation," she agreed. "The property will assuredly still be a crime scene, but hopefully the police will choose not to post a guard once their techs are finished."

"They'll take his computer." Rocky was a whiz with computers, but the chances of the cops leaving that behind were slim to none.

"They will," Kendra echoed. She relaxed in the seat, turning her attention front and center once more. "But they don't know about Yoni's backup drive or where he keeps it hidden."

Now that was a stroke of luck. "You obviously do."

"I definitely do." She shot Rocky a triumphant smile. "He recently moved it, but he gave me the location last night. Just in case."

"He was aware on some level that the threat might go beyond a reputation assassination?" In Rocky's opinion the idea that the victim felt he was in physical danger put a slightly different slant on the case.

"He didn't say as much, but I got that impression. Yoni wasn't one to break protocol.

He played by the rules." She gave Rocky another of those pointed looks. "All the rules."

Rocky studied her eyes, the certainty there, and the determined set of her jaw. "Once in a great while a true innocent is mowed down in a scenario like this, but only once in a great while. I'd wager your friend has at least one secret that'll surprise you." He didn't have to spell out the glaring fact that Sayar did not want to go to the police.

Another of those long, awkward pauses lapsed with her staring directly into his eyes.

"Maybe," she admitted.

"If I'm right, you owe me lunch." A long-awaited lunch, he didn't mention.

Her assessing gaze narrowed slightly. "You're on."

He grinned, leaned into the headrest. Lunch was a given. Rocky had never met a man or woman, dead or alive, who didn't have at least one secret. Yoni Sayar surely had his.

"If you're wrong," Kendra said, cutting into his victorious musing, "you have to wear a suit to the office every day for a week."

Surprised, he looked her straight in the eye. "Something wrong with what I wear?" He was a jeans and boots kind of guy. Sure he wore the requisite button-down shirt and sports jacket, but never suits. Well, almost never. Occasionally he had no choice.

She shook her head. "Nothing a little polish and silk won't take care of."

"Ha-ha." He pretended to be annoyed but deep down he was kind of happy that she'd bothered to observe what he wore. She sure hadn't given the first indication that she'd looked at him long enough to notice. "Nice to know you care."

"Appearances are everything, Rocky," she said, surveying the entrance to the airfield as the driver made the turn. "At the Colby Agency appearances are extremely important."

His anticipation flattened. Her attention was related to business.

Like always.

Chapter Three

Washington, D.C., Capitol Hill Diner, 1:55 p.m.

Kendra waited through the lengthy hold. When Castille's secretary returned to the line, Kendra didn't give her time to pass along the no she knew the senator had likely given. "I have to talk to him, Jean. It's urgent, as I'm sure you know."

Rocky lounged on the other side of the booth they'd claimed once the lunch crowd started to dwindle, his expression resigned to the idea that she was butting her head against a brick wall. But he had to hand it to her; she didn't give up easily.

"Kendra, I wish I could help you," Jean offered, her voice hushed. She wouldn't want to be overheard consorting with the enemy.

"I understand that an appointment is out of the question," Kendra put in before the woman who'd worked with the senator his entire senatorial career could continue, "but if you can give me some hint of his schedule for this afternoon I'll catch him on the run." Kendra had some idea of Castille's daily agenda. Two years as his personal aide had provided significant insight into his usual activities. But it had been three years.

Things changed. So did people.

"What about his three o'clock at the club?" she prodded. During Kendra's tenure as his aide, Castille hadn't missed a Wednesday afternoon sit-down with *the boys* at the club. The Summit catered to high-level D.C. politicians and businessmen, providing classic luxury along with a three hundred percent markup on beverages. Membership was required for entrance, but the sidewalk outside was fair game as long as one wasn't a reporter. If any of the old staff remained, she might just get inside. But she wasn't betting on it.

"I can't confirm that he'll make that standing appointment today, considering what's happened," Jean advised, her tone somber.

That was all Kendra needed. "Thanks, Jean. I owe you." Kendra closed her cell phone and gazed triumphantly at the man waiting across the table. "I can catch him around three." The club was barely twenty minutes away. Arriving ahead of schedule wouldn't be a problem. In fact, it might work to her advantage.

"I'm impressed. The secretary must remember you more fondly than her boss does."

Jean Brody had no children of her own. The sixty-year-old and Kendra had bonded very closely, but even that bond had never breached the woman's loyalty to the senator. What she had given today was a confirmation of something Kendra already knew. It was their mutual respect that kept Jean off Kendra's list of persons to interrogate.

As well as the knowledge that no amount of persuasion would prompt the secretary to speak ill against Castille. She was a rare breed.

"You could say that, yes," Kendra said in answer to her partner's assessment.

Rocky made an agreeable sound and resumed his monitoring of the street outside the wall of plate glass that ran the length of the diner's storefront. He was slightly out of his element but he hadn't let that cloud his attitude.

Kendra studied the man seated across the table from her. She didn't yet have a complete handle on his thought process regarding the case of her connection to the players. That he continued to act cooperatively went a long way in easing her concern about working with him. Not that he was a bad guy, he absolutely wasn't. But he was a former Equalizer and the merger with the Colby Agency had been a difficult pill to swallow to some extent for Jim Colby's entire team. Most of the bumps were behind them now.

That her attention, despite the current situation, settled on the usual details about him annoyed her, but it was what it was. An unexpected attraction that could not be allowed to proliferate.

Rocky was tall, heavily muscled. Coal-black hair and unsettlingly vivid blue eyes. Everything about him somehow refuted his background. Reared and educated in Tampa by medical professional parents, he dressed like a cowboy—sans the requisite hat. From the first time she'd met him she'd fully expected the man to drawl out a "yes, ma'am" to match that swagger of a champion that attracted the eye of every female he encountered—including Kendra's. When he walked into a room he owned it, insofar as female interest was concerned.

As if she'd made the statement out loud, her partner swung his gaze back to her.

She rerouted her thoughts. "I left a voice mail for Wayne Burton." Keep going with the details. Rocky had been in the restroom when she'd made that call. "He's a contact in D.C.'s homicide division I reached out to on occasion...before." Before she'd recognized the writing on the wall and the hard cold fact that she was not cut out for this world. And before she'd tried a relationship with him that couldn't have fit in a million years. "I'm hoping he'll agree to brief us on the path the investigation is taking at this point."

Those startlingly blue eyes searched hers a moment as if looking for the motive behind her words. "A reliable enough contact you have reason to believe he would go out on a limb to give you a break in a potentially sensitive and high-profile case?"

Rocky wasn't asking about reliability. What he had actually asked was had she slept with Wayne Burton. His eyes confirmed her analysis. "Yes," she said, unashamed. Wayne was reliable and she had slept with him. But that was history. History Leland Rockford had no need to know. She hadn't communicated with Wayne in three years...other than the occasional e-mail.

"That should make life a lot simpler." Rocky plucked a cold French fry from his plate and popped it into his mouth. "For the case anyway."

Kendra let the innuendo slide. She moistened her lips, shouldn't have stared at his, but it was difficult not to. He had very generous lips for a man. Everything about him was a contradiction. His appearance gave away nothing of his past life. His slow, methodical manner of conversing totally belied his state school academic record. The man was incredibly smart and far more insightful than he apparently wanted anyone to know, including his current partner.

And yet he didn't seem to get how this was going to play out. "Nothing about this investigation will be simple," she warned. "This is a community filled with secrets and powerful people who know how to keep the important ones—unless it benefits them somehow to share those secrets. We'll have to dig deeper and work harder for every single detail."

Rocky propped his forearms on the table and leaned forward. "Good thing neither of us is the type to surrender without a fight."

She resisted the impulse to recline deeper into the faux leather of the booth to regain those few inches of distance he had claimed. He'd done this at the hotel when he'd insisted on opening the door to her room and seeing her inside before going to his room next door. He'd gotten closer than he'd dared before, had looked her directly in the eyes and spoke quietly as if what he had to say wasn't to be overheard. That it was somehow intimate. Maybe it was her imagination but she hadn't noticed him doing that before.

She would be lying to herself if she didn't admit that he'd made her shiver. Something no other man had done with such ease.

Quite possibly she was making too much of it. She'd had zero sleep and Yoni's murder had her on an emotional ledge. She stared at her untouched food. Her appetite was AWOL. But she needed to eat. Coffee alone wouldn't keep her on her toes.

She kept replaying every moment of last

night's meeting with Yoni. What had she missed? Had he said anything at all that should have clued her in to the fact that he was in imminent danger?

How could she call herself a private investigator when she'd completely misread the urgency in a potential client she knew so well?

"You shouldn't beat yourself up."

Kendra blinked. So now he was a mind reader? "I was just—"

"Thinking how you should have seen this coming?"

Definitely a mind reader. "Maybe." Surely she'd missed something relevant in last night's meeting. Something he'd said…

"He failed to tell you everything."

She wanted to challenge that assessment. To defend her friend…she had known Yoni as well as anyone who'd worked with him could have. But logic told her that Rocky had pegged the situation. Yoni had been worried enough to contact her, to draw her from her new life. Yet he hadn't once mentioned fear for his safety…only for his professional reputation.

"It's possible he had no idea the source of the threat would go this far," she proposed. "Frankly, his murder may prove unrelated to his reasons for coming to me. There's no way to guess."

"But you don't believe that," Rocky suggested with equal conviction.

"No." Rocky was her partner in this assignment. Choosing not to be completely honest served no purpose. "I believe there is more…that he didn't tell me." It pained her to say as much, but it was true. "If that proves the case, then he had a compelling reason for leaving me in the dark." Yoni wouldn't knowingly put anyone in danger.

Rocky pulled out his wallet and dropped payment for their lunch on the table. "All we have to do is determine what that reason was."

Kendra reached for the check the waitress had left, then for her purse.

"It goes on the same expense log," Rocky reminded before sliding from the booth.

Giving herself a mental kick for again being slow on the uptake, she scooted across the bench seat and stood. "We should get into position to intercept Castille."

"Since you know the way, why don't you drive?" He gestured for her to go ahead of him.

She inhaled a whiff of his aftershave as she turned to go. The scent caught her off guard. She'd spent the last several hours in his company, seated right next to him and it wasn't until this moment she noticed the earthy masculinity of it. Despite the abundance of food smells surrounding her, his scent abruptly reached out and permeated her senses.

Sleep deprived. Frayed nerves. Too much caffeine.

After a good night's sleep she would be more herself.

But her friend would still be dead.

Summit Club, 2:50 p.m.

THE BROODING ARCHITECTURE of the exclusive club blended into the row of brick and limestone structures that flanked the tree-lined street far enough from Pennsylvania Avenue to allow some semblance of separation.

Luck appeared to be on Kendra's side as she leaned against the bar on the side of the expansive dining room opposite the lobby entrance. The afternoon shift bartender who'd worked at the club three years ago was still on staff. He'd not only allowed Kendra and Rocky inside, he'd seated them at the bar with a wide-angle view of the entrance Castille would assuredly use.

"I'm still in shock." Drea James shook his head as he checked his stock of liquors and whiskeys. "Yoni always made it a point to stop at the bar and say hello whenever he was here." Drea shrugged, the shock he spoke of evident in the listless move. "It's crazy. What's happening to this world?" He reached down for a replacement bottle of bourbon.

"Was he still dating that girl…?" Using a cliched ruse, Kendra tapped her forehead as if she was attempting to recall the name.

"Leigh?" Drea frowned. "I don't think so. He always said he was too busy for a real social life." After a moment's contemplation, he added, "She still asks about him though."

"Really?" Kendra feigned surprise. Yoni not only hadn't mentioned a girl, neither had his parents. "Maybe she hoped they would get together again."

"Wishful thinking," Drea said somberly. He glanced around, then leaned across the bar. "Don't get me wrong, Leigh's a cool chick, but Yoni was way out of her league. That dude was going places." He pointed to Rocky's glass. "More sparkling?"

Rocky held his hand over his glass. "No thanks."

The bartender turned his attention back to Kendra. "I figure that's the only reason Leigh worked so hard to get a job waitressing here. She's looking for a sugar daddy. Know what I mean?"

Definitely. "I'd like to ask her a few questions. Will she be working tonight?" Whether she was seeing Yoni now or not, anything this Leigh person had noticed or overheard could prove useful.

"Not tonight." Drea furrowed his brow thoughtfully. "Tomorrow night for sure."

"Maybe I could call her?" Kendra prodded. She wanted the woman's last name and address if she could get one or both.

Drea shook his head again. "I can't get over you being a PI now. That's wild."

"It's a different world," Kendra agreed. Telling Drea that Yoni had visited her in Chicago hadn't been on her agenda but the detail had compelled the bartender to open up. Yoni spent a lot of time in places like this meeting with colleagues and contacts. Any information she could obtain from this man might fill in numerous gaps. "The work has taught me that even the most seemingly insignificant detail can make all the difference in an investigation."

Again Drea appeared to contemplate her words. As if he'd suddenly remembered something he picked up a pen and grabbed a cocktail napkin. "This is Leigh's cell number." He scribbled on the napkin.

"And her address." He pushed the napkin across the bar. "You tell her I said she needs to share anything she knows with you."

Kendra read the name. Leigh Turlington. "Thanks. This helps a lot." She gave the bartender a smile as she withdrew a business card from her purse and presented it to him. "And you call me if you hear anything at all related to Yoni."

Drea examined the card. "You know I will."

"Right on time," Rocky said under his breath.

Kendra followed his gaze to the mirror behind the bar. The reflection of the room behind them showed Castille and two other men following the hostess to a table near one of the towering windows with a view of the street below. For added privacy, the dining room was located on the second floor.

"He only allows one member of his security inside," Drea explained, keeping his voice hushed. "He's the one in the black suit. The other guy is Bernard Capshaw. He's the CEO of Capshaw Enterprises."

A waitress approached the other end of the bar, drawing Drea in that direction.

Kendra wasn't acquainted with Capshaw the man, but she knew the company. Aerospace technology. The industry, like many others, was on the edge of financial collapse and in need of government support.

Castille hadn't changed much. If anything he looked younger. The wonders of modern cosmetic procedures. She couldn't see the man going for full-blown surgery but there were other, more convenient procedures that provided ample benefits.

Appearances were supremely important in this high-stakes arena.

The other man, Secret Service no doubt, was an unknown to her. No one from three years ago but that changed nothing. Kendra was well aware of SOP. The senator wouldn't be allowed out of the man's line of sight except to visit the men's room and only then after the facility had been checked for hidden threats.

"I'll be waiting in the ladies' room," Kendra said to Rocky. "Send me a text if Castille wanders in that direction."

"You might be in for a long wait," Rocky noted.

That was true, but it was the only way to ensure she got one-on-one time with the senator. And that she didn't attract the attention of his security. "Text me if he leaves the table."

"Will do."

Rocky watched her in the mirror behind the bar as she slid off the stool. As she made her way to the ladies' room she wondered how long his total cooperation would last. So far he hadn't actually questioned any of her decisions, but then they'd scarcely begun.

The ladies' room had been renovated since Kendra's last visit here. Opulence remained the mainstay of the decorating theme. Nothing but the best for the power players. At one point some newly elected senator had suggested that popular gathering spots like the Summit were subsidized by wealthy lobbyists who wanted the atmosphere conducive to persuasion.

No one paid any real attention to the accusation, yet everyone understood that it was in all likelihood true on some level.

Money talked.

Most anything else walked.

Kendra's cell vibrated in its leather holster. She checked the display. The text was from Rocky and read: Security headed your way.

The man in the black suit would check the men's room then return to the table to let the senator know it was all clear. Since both the men's room and the ladies' were stationed in a short corridor that led to nothing else, entry was possible only from the dining room. Permitting security to feel comfortable allowing the man to do his business in private.

Let me know when security returns to the table and Castille heads this way, she entered before hitting the send button.

Kendra checked her reflection. Smoothed a hand over her suit jacket. She looked as tired as she felt. The weariness particularly showed in her eyes. Never a good position from which to strike. This would be her first face-to-face with Castille since the day she'd walked out of his office. He wouldn't be happy to see her.

"Tough," she muttered.

Her cell vibrated. Security has returned to table. Your mark is en route.

Kendra tucked her phone away and took a breath. She pressed her ear to the door and listened for the neighboring hinges to whine. The carpeted floor prevented her from hearing Castille's approach.

A soft metal-on-metal rub signaled the senator had entered the men's room directly across the narrow corridor. Time to move.

She eased open the ladies' room door and quickly surveyed the corridor all the while knowing that Rocky would have warned her if anyone else had approached the area.

Clear.

Though no one had come this way while they sat at the bar, she still felt uncomfortable barging into the men's room. Putting manners aside, she crossed the corridor in two strides and entered forbidden territory.

Castille stood before the row of marble sinks admiring his thick head of gray hair in the mirror. Apparently satisfied, he reached to adjust his silk jacket. As the door whooshed closed behind Kendra his gaze collided with hers in the mirror.

"Afternoon, Senator." Kendra closed in on his position, her head held high, her shoulders square.

He stilled. Fury flared in his eyes. *"You."*

That he didn't immediately go for the call button on the belt at his waist surprised her. Security would have descended upon the men's room in ten seconds or less. And she would be spending hours under federal interrogation.

"It's been a while," she commented as she leaned one hip against the cool marble about three feet from where he stood. Crowding him wasn't the goal.

He cut her a look that warned exactly

how he still felt about her. "I don't know what you think you're doing, but you're making a very serious error in judgment. This is stalking."

"Yoni was my friend." That his primary worry was her presence infuriated Kendra. "I want to know what happened to him."

"His murder," Castille said in a matter-of-fact tone, "had nothing to do with his work." His attention shifted back to the mirror as he straightened his purple tie yet again. "You should have checked your facts before you bothered to make an appearance."

"Why don't you enlighten me?" she suggested while he openly admired the fit of his charcoal suit.

He faced her, the lack of compassion in his expression fueling her fury. "The official conclusion at this point is that the homicide that occurred early this morning had nothing to do with Sayar's political position. Preliminary results of the homicide investigation will be released tomorrow morning. You, like the rest of the world, can catch it on your preferred news channel."

"He came to me with concerns," she countered. Let him offer an explanation for that. "I'm here to follow up on those concerns."

Castille puffed. "Yoni was losing his edge. Confidence in his ability was on a downward trend. Surely you haven't forgotten how it works in this town. There are two kinds of folks."

The bastard took the time to wash his hands before continuing. Kendra's fury rushed unimpeded toward the boiling point.

Castille selected a meticulously rolled hand towel from the basket on the counter and dried his hands then settled his condescending gaze upon her once more. "Those who rise to the mountaintop and those who tumble over the edge of the cliff. Yoni was stumbling. He was on his way down. There was nothing I could do to help him."

"Because of the Transparency Bill?"

The brief glimmer of surprise in those

cold eyes sent triumph rocketing into her chest. He knew Kendra well enough to understand that if she knew that, she knew much more.

"The bill is brilliant," Castille confessed. "But the weight of taking such a stand helped to push our friend off that ledge, Kendra. The pressure under these kinds of circumstances is immeasurable. Yoni buckled under that tremendous weight."

The senator shrugged. "There is no mystery here. Tomorrow's press conference will set the record straight for any conspiracy theorists. Such as yourself," he accused.

"I'll make my own determination as to whether there's a mystery or not," she challenged, not put off one bit by his condescension. She wasn't going anywhere until she had the whole truth.

"Then consider yourself on notice." Castille tossed the hand towel aside. "If you attempt to connect Yoni's troubles to me or my office, you will be profoundly sorry you made the mistake of coming back."

He walked past her.

"Consider yourself on notice, Senator." She turned, surprised that he'd hesitated at the door, his back to her. "I'm not afraid of you or your position. If the facts lead back to you, that's where I'll go. And *if* that's the case, you will be the one profoundly sorry."

He opened the door and walked out, the whoosh of the closing door underscoring his departure.

The gauntlet was on the ground.

Let the battle of wills commence.

Chapter Four

Judd Castille glowered at the lobby entrance long after Kendra and her cohort had departed.

He should have known Sayar would go to her. Judd had kept up with the self-righteous witch in part because of Sayar's occasional comment in regards to her professional rise in the field of private investigations. She had landed herself a position at a widely acclaimed agency. But Judd hadn't cared. He'd only been thankful she was out of his hair. She had been a thorn in his side the last year of her tenure with him.

Now she was back.

And it was that nervous fool Sayar's fault.

Judd had actually expected her to show

up after hearing the news of her friend's murder. However, he certainly hadn't expected her to have the unmitigated gall to confront him on his own turf. Who did Kendra Todd think she was?

She was no one.

No one who mattered.

"Is there a problem, Senator?"

Judd shifted his attention to the man seated next to him. "Why would there be a problem?" The situation with Capshaw was precarious enough without an appearance from the likes of Kendra Todd. Distraction could crush a man's best efforts. Judd could not allow anything or anyone to distract him at this pivotal juncture.

Far too much was at stake. Sayar had recognized that immensity, as well. What had he been thinking going to Kendra?

"You seem distracted," Capshaw offered, a hint of victory already shining in his beady eyes.

"And rightly so," Judd returned, restraining the infinite derision he felt for the man. "Yoni Sayar was murdered this morning.

He was a trusted colleague. He'll be greatly missed."

Capshaw sipped his scotch—scotch paid for by Judd and ultimately the taxpayers. "I'm not so sure the architecture of the Transparency Bill will withstand this tragic loss."

As if the bastard gave one damn. Again, Judd curbed his baser urges, like reaching across the table and strangling the man. "I have full confidence the bill will be moving forward." If it was the last thing Judd did, he would get that piece of legislation passed. Men like Capshaw proved all the motivation necessary.

This vicious cycle had to stop.

Regret trickled through him but he banished it. He would not permit failure.

Truth was Judd was tired. Feeling his age. At sixty-three he had one or two more terms at most in him. He needed to leave his mark. To accomplish something that would put him in the history books.

He was on the verge of doing exactly that…if he could keep Kendra Todd out of his way until this ugliness passed. She would stir the pot…make things worse.

Confidence welled inside him. He had a plan in place to divert her attentions. By the time she recognized that she was on a path going nowhere, Judd's position as an American hero would be sealed.

His gaze settled on Capshaw as the greedy bastard scanned the menu. And men like him would no longer be able to steal from the ordinary citizens of this country to feather their own nests.

This was a war. Sacrifices had to be made.

If Kendra wasn't careful she could very well join others already on that casualty list.

Chapter Five

Crystal City, 5:20 p.m.

"When we get inside, I'll keep him talking while you look around."

"Got it." The lady had moxie, Rocky had to give her that. The meeting with Castille had visibly shaken her but she'd come right out of that confrontation ready to move on to the next step. She'd put a call in to Leigh Turlington, a woman Sayar had dated. But it turned up to be a dead end. They'd only gone on one date and Turlington hadn't even known Sayar's phone number, much less what he was into.

Rocky had offered to drive from the Summit to Yoni Sayar's residence just outside Crystal City, allowing Kendra time to decompress rather than fight rush-hour traffic.

Yellow crime-scene tape draped the sidewalk and small patch of grass in front of the town house, a blatant warning that bad things had happened on the other side. In this case, Sayar had been shot as he started up the short walk from the street to his front door. At least that was the story they'd gotten from the grieving parents. No official word had been released by the local authorities. According to Castille that wouldn't happen until tomorrow morning. Unless Kendra could get something out of the guy they were waiting for.

Rocky had parked across the street from the victim's residence. The late afternoon sun glinted against the windows of the two-story home. Wide brick steps led to the nondescript front door. Rocky squinted at first one window then the next. All appeared to be closed up right with blinds or shutters. No sign of the cops or any lingering crime-scene technicians.

"Your friend is late," he noted aloud as

Kendra checked the time on her cell phone yet again.

"He's a homicide detective," she reminded Rocky, her own impatience showing. "I'm certain sticking to a time schedule isn't always his top priority." She returned her attention to the town house that had belonged to her friend. "Wayne will be here."

Wayne. That was right, they were friends, too. Rocky had his own theory about that particular friend. He'd picked up on the subtle change in the inflections of her voice when she'd spoken to her *contact.* Not that it was any of his business, personally or professionally, or his concern insofar as this case stacked up or how they conducted their investigation.

The concept just bugged him.

No use denying it...the idea of Kendra and another man, any man, got under his skin somehow. Didn't seem to matter that they hardly knew each other beyond the workplace. Dumb, yeah. But a fact nonetheless. He'd learned at an early age that denial was less than constructive and totally unproductive.

A black SUV rolled to a stop in front of the town house. The driver's door opened and a tall man wearing a suit stepped out.

Had to be Burton. *Her contact.* Rocky disliked him already, mostly because of the suit.

"That's him," Kendra reached for her door.

Rocky did the same, giving her ample time to round the hood across the street ahead of him. Kendra hadn't mentioned whether she'd informed Burton she was bringing along a partner.

Waiting through the requisite embrace, Rocky stood back until the reunion formalities were out of the way. *"It's been forever." "God, you look good."* He rolled his eyes. Primarily because Burton had it right. Kendra did look good.

Rocky closed the final couple of yards between his position and theirs. Burton dragged his focus from the lady and pointed it at Rocky. Rocky stuck out his hand. "Leland Rockford," he announced.

Burton gave Rocky's hand a challenging but brisk shake. "Lieutenant Wayne Burton, D.C. Homicide."

Maybe he misheard but Rocky could swear the man had emphasized the lieutenant part. Rocky jerked his head toward Kendra. "Her partner."

Burton ignored that last part, resting his attention on Kendra once more. "You may have been the last person to see Sayar alive," he said as he turned to the town house, placed a hand at the small of her back and ushered her in that direction.

Rocky bit back the compulsion to say "Besides the folks at two airports and the car rental agency." Just another reason he didn't like the guy. Another dumb reason.

Except that Kendra looked at Burton as if every word coming from his mouth were the gospel that would show her the way to the promised land. He couldn't recall once having her look at him that way.

Burton lifted the official crime-scene

tape for Kendra to duck beneath. Once on the other side, they walked wide around the bloodstained section on the walk where the victim had fallen. At the stoop the overly friendly detective removed the crime-scene seal from the door and unlocked it.

Rocky stayed two steps behind. He figured he would learn more by watching and listening than by attempting to insert himself into the conversation.

Kendra moved slowly around the living room, visually inspecting the space. She'd told Rocky that she'd been here before and hopefully would recognize anything glaringly out of place.

"So Sayar didn't give you any details about why he wanted to hire your agency?" Burton asked.

For a second Rocky was sure he'd misunderstood the question.

"He promised to give me all the details when I arrived in D.C. tomorrow," Kendra said, clearing the confusion for Rocky. She turned to face Burton. "That was to be our first official meeting."

Rocky restrained the smile that tugged at the corners of his mouth. The lady wasn't as smitten as he'd first thought. She'd kept the details of the final conversation with Sayar to herself. Good deal.

"He simply said," she added, "that it was urgent and personal."

Burton assessed her at length, obviously not fully buying her story. "He came all that way and didn't give you anything?"

She moved to the table next to a recliner and bent down to view the framed photo there. "He said he couldn't discuss the situation by phone. Showing up to talk to me was his only choice. He wanted a commitment from me that the Colby Agency would take his case and then we would move forward." She straightened and looked Burton straight in the eye and lied. "He wasn't willing to share anything until I had the backing of the agency."

Rocky was impressed.

"Puts a whole new spin on what we know."

Kendra inclined her head and studied her old friend. “What exactly do you know?”

“Allowing you and your partner access to the property is breaking the rules,” Burton hedged.

“The techs have finished,” Kendra challenged.

“You wouldn’t be here otherwise,” Burton tossed right back.

“Touché,” Kendra conceded.

This part Rocky was enjoying more and more.

“What I’m about to tell you won’t be released until tomorrow morning’s press conference,” Burton began. “I’m counting on you” he glanced at Rocky with no lack of suspicion “to keep this quiet until then.”

“You have our word,” Kendra assured him.

A brief hesitation no doubt for the effect, then Burton announced, “We have evidence the shooting was the result of Sayar surprising a burglar.”

Rocky hadn’t noticed any sign of forced access at the front door.

"Solid evidence?" Kendra wanted to know.

Rocky decided to wander around the room as the two hashed out the theory. That was the plan Kendra had laid out. All indications so far suggested that Sayar lived frugally, Rocky decided. Minimal furnishings. Minimal decorating. Nothing on the walls except a calendar over the desk. No laptop or desktop sat on the desk, confirming Rocky's conjecture that the police would have confiscated it right away.

"His wallet was missing as were his computer and a flat-panel television that hung over the mantel." He pointed to the fireplace.

Rocky's attention moved from the cop to the mantel and back. So, the techs hadn't gotten the computer. Interesting. Maybe Sayar's murder was a coincidence after all. Part of a robbery. It wasn't totally outside the realm of possibility.

Just highly unlikely considering his meeting with Kendra.

While Kendra launched more questions

at Burton, Rocky seized the opportunity to drift into the kitchen. Dirty dishes in the sink, despite the built-in dishwasher. Counters were clear of clutter except for a can opener and a microwave. Stove top and oven looked unused.

Rocky opened the fridge. Carton of milk and orange juice. Sandwich meat, which was out of date. Same with the cheese. Freezer compartment was empty.

A few cans of soup in the cabinets. One half-empty box of crackers.

A definite bachelor.

Rocky listened to ensure there had been no break in the conversation in the other room, then checked the back door. Again, no indication of forced entry. When he eased it closed once more, he didn't lock it.

Just in case.

With Kendra and Burton still deep in intense conversation, Rocky moved to the only other room downstairs. The bathroom. Toilet paper and hand soap. Pedestal sink and toilet. Empty medicine cabinet. Like the rest of the walls downstairs, a generic shade of off-white coated the walls and trim. Floors were covered with faux-wood flooring.

A cell phone erupted into chimes. Rocky stopped in the tiny square of a hall between the living room and bath to listen. Burton reached into his jacket pocket and then his gruff voice replaced the chimes. Kendra's gaze collided with Rocky's as he approached the stairs leading to the second floor. Her nod of encouragement was so subtle had he not been staring so intently at her he would have missed it entirely.

She would keep Burton occupied.

By the time Rocky had reached the upstairs landing Burton had ended the call. Kendra tossed out another demand for information.

Upstairs four doors lined a short, narrow hall, two on either side. The beige carpet hushed Rocky's footfalls. Door one led to a bedroom furnished with only a futon. Nothing in the closet. Doors two and three opened to a bathroom and a linen closet respectively. The final door opened into the bedroom Sayar had used.

More of the generic paint. Double bed with tousled linens. Clothes hung neatly in the closet. Shoes lined the floor beneath. One chest of drawers with a flat-panel TV resting on top. Rocky quickly and efficiently rifled through each drawer. Socks, T-shirts, boxers. That was about it.

He lifted the mattress from the box springs. Nothing under the mattress. He knelt down. Or under the bed. A few magazines, an MP3 player and two framed photos cluttered the bedside table. Along with a couple of twenty-dollar bills. Seemed a little strange that a burglar would leave cash lying around.

The drawers of the bedside table contained the usual suspects: tissue, throat lozenges and a flashlight. The only thing missing was a pack of condoms. Most single guys kept those handy.

Before exiting the room, Rocky stood back and took one last look around.

Then it hit him.

There were several items in the room that shouldn't have been if Burton's theory was to be accepted.

Rocky didn't bother quieting his steps as he descended the stairs. Burton shot him a harsh glare but couldn't drag himself away from the conversation with Kendra long enough to reprimand Rocky.

"I'm not buying the robbery theory," Kendra argued. "He was far too agitated last night. Something was very wrong in his life. Seems one hell of a coincidence that he was murdered a few hours later practically at his own door."

Burton flared his palms. "Our only option is to go with the evidence we find. Unless we discover some additional information that suggests otherwise our hands are tied. The case will be written up as a robbery-homicide."

"And go unsolved like the hundreds of others that occur in your jurisdiction every year."

Now that was cutting the guy off at the knees. This was the first time Rocky had watched Kendra in action out in the field. So far he continued to be impressed.

Another of those annoyed glances arrowed Rocky's way. Rocky hadn't made a peep. Apparently the cop in his fancy suit didn't like being dressed down by his former girlfriend in front of her new male partner.

Burton dropped his hands to his sides and said nothing in response to her accusation. "Is there anything else here you want to see that" he cut Rocky another look "you haven't already?"

Kendra met Rocky's gaze, he shook his head, then she said to Burton, "I guess that's it."

When they were on the street once more Burton exhaled a big breath. "Look, I'll keep you posted. There'll be a final decision later tonight before we go public tomorrow morning."

"I really appreciate your support, Wayne."

Rocky headed for the rental car. Kendra knew what she was doing. If she needed some space to get what she needed from this guy, Rocky wasn't going to stand in her way.

The investigation was top priority.

Still, he couldn't help looking back as he reached the car. Burton gave Kendra another of those big hugs, only this time he held on a little longer than before.

Rocky hit unlock on the remote and got behind the wheel. That part he didn't need to observe.

He stared at his reflection in the rearview mirror. *Man, you are getting desperate way before your time.*

If Kendra Todd was into him he would know it by now. She wasn't. He needed to get that through his thick skull and focus on the case.

Kendra hurried across the street and to the passenger side. When she'd settled into the seat she smiled. "Drive around the neighborhood."

"Yes, ma'am." He started the car, waited until Burton had driven away and then eased from the curb. “Any particular reason or are we just checking out the architecture?”

“I need to get to the patio.”

“For?” Rocky made a left at the first intersection.

“That’s where Yoni told me he’d hidden his backup hard drive.”

“If the cops didn’t find it,” Rocky countered.

“Trust me, they didn’t find it.”

Sayar must have had one hell of a good hiding place. “What’s your take on the robbery scenario?”

“No way,” Kendra said with absolute certainty. “Someone wanted it to look that way.”

“I don’t think the cops are buying it, either.” He slowed for another turn, this one right. “Not for real. If they are, then they’re not too bright.”

Kendra turned in her seat to study him. “What did you see in the other rooms besides Yoni’s lack of decorating skills?”

She had that part right. “I’m guessing he ate out a lot.”

She smiled, her expression—her eyes—distant. Rocky's throat tightened. The smile hadn't been for him but he'd liked it a lot all the same. "He ate out and with his parents. Cooking was not one of his fortes."

"No beer or hard stuff, either."

"Focused and unusually straitlaced."

Rocky felt a twinge of sympathy for the parents. They had raised a good, hardworking son it seemed and this happened to him. Not fair. Not fair at all.

"What about his bedroom?"

"Now there," Rocky made another slow turn, "is where things got interesting." He rolled carefully past a house where children played kick ball in the yard. "Sayar's wallet and computer were missing. But not the thirty-two-inch flat-panel television in his bedroom. An MP3 player lay right on the bedside table in plain sight. No cheapo, either. This was one of the high-dollar jobs. And if that isn't enough to convince you this was no robbery, forty bucks was next to the MP3 player."

"I knew Wayne was holding out on me."

Kendra shook her head, her lips compressed in a firm line.

"That's his job," Rocky offered. He had no idea why he felt compelled to defend the guy, but it was a reasonable explanation.

Kendra opened her mouth to argue, but then snapped it shut.

Didn't take a mind reader to know what she'd started to say. She had expected more from her former lover. Maybe the two had been a lot closer than Rocky had suspected.

"I suppose the burglar could have been interrupted by Yoni's return before he made it to the second floor," Kendra suggested, playing devil's advocate.

"Possibly," Rocky agreed. "But if he had that much notice that Sayar was coming, why not run out the back door and avoid the whole confrontation?"

"Exactly," Kendra agreed.

No way it was a robbery.

"There's an alley between the rows of town houses," Kendra said, "take the one directly behind Yoni's side of the street."

Rocky doubled back, then maneuvered down the narrow alley, careful of the garbage cans and bicycles. Each town house had a privacy fenced patio area and a parking pad designed for two vehicles.

"That's Yoni's car." Kendra pointed to the next parking pad on the left.

Rocky pulled in beside the small green hybrid. "He must have taken a taxi to the airport and then back." Otherwise he would have entered his home from the back door."

"Makes sense."

Kendra was out of the car as soon as Rocky had shifted into Park. As he emerged from the vehicle she lifted the latch on the gate and disappeared behind the eight-foot dog-eared fence.

Rocky scanned the alley. A cat pilfered through an open garbage can a few houses down. Otherwise the alley was quiet and vacant.

Satisfied that Burton or one of his buddies wasn't going to show up and arrest them for breaking and entering, Rocky stepped through the gate she'd left standing open. He'd expected to find her moving patio chairs or prowling through the two shrubs flanking either side of the steps leading to the back door.

He hadn't anticipated finding her dismantling the barbecue grill. She'd opened the lid, removed the rack and was digging through the mound of unused charcoal.

Rocky was just about to ask her what she hoped to find when she produced a large zip plastic bag. Inside was a square boxlike device.

Kendra turned to him with victory on her lips. "Yoni's external hard drive."

Like he realized earlier, the lady had moxie.

Rocky re-mounded the charcoal, replaced the rack and closed the lid. He couldn't help eyeing the windows of the town house as he dusted his palms together. "We should get moving."

"I'll hook this up to my laptop when we get back to the hotel." Dirty bag or not,

Kendra stashed her find beneath her cream-colored jacket.

"We don't need back inside for anything, right?"

She shook her head.

Being a good citizen and because Burton would know who'd unlocked the back door, Rocky locked it, then checked to ensure it was secure. No need to tick off Kendra's one official *contact*.

The alley was still deserted except for that determined cat who'd found himself an edible treasure. Once in the rental car, Rocky resisted the impulse to zoom away from the scene of their crime. Drawing unnecessary attention wouldn't be smart.

Kendra tucked the bag with its contents beneath her seat and reached for her seat belt. She hesitated, then reached for her cell phone.

"Kendra Todd."

The sound of her name made him smile. When he'd first learned that the Equalizers would be joining the Colby Agency he'd had some reservations. But now, after getting to know the staff—Kendra in particular—Rocky felt pretty much at home.

"Who is this?"

Rocky shifted his attention to her as he braked for the first intersection.

Kendra drew the phone from her ear and stared at the screen.

"What's up?" Tension rifled through Rocky.

Her gaze connected with his. "We have a rendezvous where we'll supposedly receive evidence about Yoni's murder and the identity of the killer."

Rocky checked the cross street then pulled away from the intersection. "Your caller didn't ID himself?"

"No."

The single syllable carried a truckload of confusion and disbelief.

"Did he name Sayar's killer just now?"

"Yes."

Their gazes intersected once more.

"Senator Castille."

Chapter Six

Lincoln Memorial, 9:00 p.m.

Kendra waited in the shadows of the Lincoln Memorial. Yoni Sayar deserved justice. Having his death swept under the rug as a random act of violence was wrong. Kendra intended to right that wrong.

"We've got company," Rocky whispered in her ear via the communications link.

"Black sedan," she confirmed.

Room service at the hotel had provided the fuel she'd been lacking. With no sleep, she'd been on the verge of total exhaustion. But the anonymous call along with a ham and cheese on rye back at the room had energized her. With Rocky's help she'd spent two hours attempting to make some sense of Yoni's electronic files. Her friend hadn't warned her that the files would be encrypted.

Why would he ensure she knew where his external hard drive was hidden if she couldn't make sense of the information stored there? Rocky had downloaded the files and sent them to the Colby Agency for further attempts at decoding. Two staff members from research were pulling an all-nighter toward that end.

She and Rocky had assessed their needs and selected the essential equipment, including their weapons, for this covert rendezvous. Arriving an hour early had provided the opportunity to survey the area and get into place. The minutes had dragged by like hours. Exhaustion had crept back into Kendra's bones.

A man emerged from the sedan she'd spotted and headed for the steps leading to the monument. He carried a slim briefcase or portfolio. Kendra checked the weapon at the small of her back beneath her jacket. Whatever this guy's game, she was prepared. Rocky was less than ten feet away, lost in the shadows, as well.

Before the man reached the top of the steps he reached up and ran a hand—his left hand—through his hair. Irritation burned through Kendra. She stepped forward, allowing her anonymous caller to see her.

Grant Roper.

Castille's aide. Kendra's replacement. Left-handed, arrogant, conniving jerk.

The surprise she'd felt at having the anonymous caller name Castille as Yoni's killer evolved into equal measures of astonishment and outrage. Roper had been bucking for her position for months before she'd walked away. What the hell was he doing turning on the man he idolized now? This did not feel right.

The distinct hum of a setup vibrated the night air.

"Kendra," Grant acknowledged as he stepped closer.

"I don't know why you called and asked for this meeting." Kendra took another step in his direction, giving him her most intimidating glower. "But I don't appreciate your games, Grant. Good night."

She stared past him.

"I told you I have evidence. Do you want to see it or not?"

The question stopped Kendra's determined departure. She turned her head to stare at him over her shoulder. "Did Castille send you?" That would be just like the old buzzard to send his minion to try and spy on Kendra's investigation. He would know all the right buzz words that would get her attention.

Grant's face furrowed into an incredulous mix of shock and desperation. "Are you joking? He'd have the same thing done to me that he did to Sayar if he even suspected I was talking to you."

"Why should I believe anything you say?" Kendra contested. He'd have to do more than talk if he wanted her to be swayed. She didn't trust him one iota. "Where's the evidence you claim to have?"

He jerked his head to the left. "Let's move away from these spotlights."

Kendra gestured for him to go first. He'd barely taken two steps before Rocky moved out of the shadows. Grant balked.

"Who's he?"

"My partner." Kendra moved in closer. "That's all you need to know. Now, let's see that evidence or I am out of here."

Grant was visibly displeased with Rocky's presence but that was too bad. Kendra had absolutely no sympathy for the slimy little snake.

He pulled a manila folder from his leather case. "I can show you what I have, but I can't let these originals out of my possession. Castille thinks I destroyed them. If he finds out…"

Yeah, Kendra got the idea but that didn't mean she believed a word of what Grant had to say. She accepted the folder. It felt heavier than it looked. She opened it, stared at the first of what turned out to be a stack of eight-by-ten photos. There were six in all. Each one showed Senator Castille in intimate conversation if not compromising positions with a young woman. Judging by the way she was dressed, a prostitute.

"Who's the woman?" Kendra banished her own conclusion and focused on Grant's face, looking for the signs of deception she fully expected.

"She *was* Aleesha Ferguson. Spent most of her time working K and L Streets. When she wasn't serving the senator's needs—if you know what I mean."

Kendra shook her head. "I find this difficult to believe." Had to be a hoax. She thrust the folder back at the man she knew from experience would beg, borrow or steal to get what he wanted. "Castille is a lot of things but not this."

"I've been keeping tabs on his extracurricular activity for months," Grant argued. "This is no one-time occurrence. The pictures are real."

"You said *was*." Kendra waited while Grant put the folder away then met her gaze. "What happened to this Aleesha Ferguson?"

"Hit-and-run." Grant lifted his chin and

stared knowingly at Kendra. "Your friend Sayar helped cover up the whole thing."

The little weasel had crossed the line with that statement. "Yoni would never have knowingly participated in a criminal act of any sort." Kendra made up her mind. "We're done."

She turned her back on the wannabe player and headed for the steps. Rocky moved up beside her, adjusting his stride to hers.

"Check it out," Grant called out to her. "Aleesha Ferguson was killed by a hit-and-run driver. The case was never solved. Mrs. Castille was the driver. She called Sayar that night. Check his cell phone records. You'll see!"

"I'm telling you the truth!" floated across the summer air as Kendra reached the car.

Rocky started the engine and roared away from the curb. Kendra steamed, so angry she barely remembered to fasten her seat belt.

"Any possibility that twerp is telling some fragment of truth?"

Kendra wanted to say unequivocally hell no. No way would Castille stoop to such immoral behavior. Absolutely no way would Yoni help anyone—not even Mrs. Castille, who, he undeniably admired and adored—cover up a murder. No. No. No.

"The pictures were real," Kendra confessed. Whatever else she didn't understand or want to believe, that much was jarringly bona fide. "But there may be a perfectly logical explanation we're not aware of." There had to be one. She couldn't wrap her head around the outrageous concept otherwise.

"Then we have to make ourselves aware."

Kendra met Rocky's unrelenting gaze. Her partner was right. No one was going to willingly give them any facsimile of the truth about Yoni's murder or anything else, for that matter, he may or may not have been involved in personally or professionally.

Not here...where secrecy and diversion were ways of life.

10:31 p.m.

KENDRA INSERTED THE KEYCARD into the door of her hotel room. She would definitely need coffee to stay focused while they hashed through the pathetic clues and leads they had at this point.

"I'll grab my laptop," Rocky said as he unlocked the door directly across the hall.

"I'll put on a pot of coffee." Kendra pushed through the door, flipped the light switch and tossed her purse onto the luggage rack.

Instinct nudged her, sending her gaze sweeping across the room. Her breath stalled in her chest.

"What the...?"

Her room had been ransacked.

The side chair's upholstery was shredded. The mattress tossed off the bed... linens strewn across the carpet. Drawers had been removed from the chest and scattered haphazardly on the floor.

Her attention settled next on the travel bag she'd abandoned when they first arrived, its contents seemingly vomited from the zippered opening.

The external hard drive.

She stumbled across the room in her haste. Dropping to her knees at the desk, she crawled beneath it and peered up at the under side of the desk top.

The compact piece of hardware was gone.

Kendra eased back from under the desk and plopped down cross-legged on the carpet. Something else she should have anticipated. Castille knew she was here. Wayne. She couldn't see what Wayne had to gain by taking the drive. Castille...the jury was still out on him.

Okay, it wasn't a total disaster, she reminded herself. Rocky had downloaded the files and forwarded all to the Colby Agency. So nothing was actually lost in that sense.

The problem was that now someone had their hands on Yoni's files. The ones he'd wanted to ensure she alone found if anything happened to him.

The most she could hope for at this point was that the agency could break the encryption before whoever had taken the external drive did so.

A long, low whistle reverberated from the door.

She looked up as her partner entered the criminal disarray. "I think it's safe to say someone suspected Yoni had discussed more with you than the idea of hiring the Colby Agency."

"Only two people were aware of my meeting with Yoni," she voiced the theories she had already considered.

"Castille could have sent his underling to distract you while another of his loyal followers did this," Rocky theorized.

"But," Kendra argued, "I'm one hundred percent certain he wouldn't have sent those pictures as a prop."

"That leaves Burton."

"Yeah," she granted.

Would Wayne have given her and Rocky access to Yoni's home if he was building a cover-up? Rocky had ensured they hadn't been tailed after they'd left Yoni's town house.

On the other hand, would her old friend have permitted their entrance into the crime scene—which was unquestionably outside regulations—for this very purpose? To determine if she knew something he didn't... like where the external hard drive was?

Kendra didn't want to believe the worst about him. Like Yoni, she'd always considered Wayne one of the good guys. Even a good man had his price. Castille was immensely powerful. Not that he'd proven a particularly bad guy, but power often brought out the worst in a person. The senator was no exception.

She rubbed her eyes, pushed her hair back. This was exactly why she'd left this world behind.

No one could be trusted when professional gain was at stake.

"Damn it." Kendra braced to get up when a hand reached down to her. She looked from the strong, wide hand to the man standing over her.

"Come on." He wiggled his fingers. "We'll move across the hall and use my laptop. See what we can find out about this Aleesha Ferguson. We'll figure this out," he hitched his head toward the mess, "later."

Kendra placed her hand in his, watched as his long fingers curled around hers. Warmth whispered through her, bringing with it a sense of relief and safety she needed more than she would dare say out loud.

Rocky pulled her to her feet in one smooth motion. "Housekeeping will take care of the mess." He gestured to the room at large and shrugged. "It's not so bad."

Another reality settled in as Kendra took a closer inventory of the room. No, it wasn't bad, the place was a disaster. Curtains, linens, furnishings had been damaged or destroyed. Hotel management was not going to be happy when they saw this.

"Okay," she relented. He was thinking a lot more clearly than she was. Kendra felt so damned tired. So frustrated. Her soul ached with regret for Yoni…for his family.

And her heart twisted with the need to find the truth…and justice.

Rocky kept her hand in his, leading the way to the door. As she stepped over her scattered clothing she hesitated, frowned. Pulling free of Rocky's gentle hold, she crouched down to inspect her favorite teal blouse. Shredded…like the chair. One piece at a time she picked up each item she'd hastily packed. Every single one was damaged beyond repair. Except the pair of jeans and the T-shirt she'd thrown in for no real reason. Maybe to blend better with her partner.

Didn't matter. Just clothes. She could buy more.

Why would whoever had come here looking for the hard drive have done this?

This part was a personal attack against her.

Rocky ushered her to her feet once more. "Don't let this scare tactic get to you. The person or persons responsible want you to be afraid."

He was right. She nodded, then followed

him out the door, grabbing her purse as she went. Her attempts at slowing the whirlwind of confusion building to a hurricane in her brain proved impotent.

Searching for the external drive, then taking it, she could see. Someone had something to hide and didn't want her to find it.

But why the personal attack?

Maybe just the fear factor, like Rocky had said. Probably not personal at all. Well, whoever had damaged her things could get over it. She wasn't going anywhere. Not even across the street to another hotel. She and Rocky were showing no fear. This reaction from the enemy proved one thing for certain: someone was getting nervous.

When they were in Rocky's room, door closed and locked, he pointed to the chair, a duplicate of the damaged one in hers, and ordered: "Sit. I'll make coffee."

Kendra couldn't say how many minutes passed with her brain meandering in a shocked daze, but the smell of freshly brewed coffee drew her mind back to the here and now. "Smells good," she had the presence of mind to say.

"I don't know about good," Rocky said as he handed her a cup, "but definitely strong."

She cradled the cup in both hands, letting the heat permeate her palms. Felt comforting.

Rocky sat down at the desk and fired up his laptop. "Is that *A-l-i-s-h-a* Ferguson?"

"Try that," Kendra suggested. "If you don't get the right hit, go for *A-l-e-e-s-h-a*." She sipped her coffee, her mind replaying the images from the photos. Castille in a car with the Ferguson woman. The two in what looked to be an alleyway. Always at night. Always alone. Always deep in conversation.

But never touching or kissing…

If Castille was having an affair wouldn't whoever snapped the candid shots have caught at least one image of that behavior?

"Aleesha with the two *e*'s," Rocky confirmed. "Twenty-two. No known next-of-kin. Investigators deemed her the victim of a hit-and-run that occurred sometime between midnight and 3:00 a.m. on June 2. No suspects as of the date of this article. Maryland native. That's about it. The woman in the article photo definitely looks like the one in the shots Roper showed off."

Kendra fished for her cell phone and put a call into the agency. After giving a condensed briefing of the day's events, researcher Patsy Talley promised to do all she could to get Yoni Sayar's cell phone records for the past two months and to look into Aleesha Ferguson's background and death. Kendra thanked her colleague and ended the call.

"Anything else?" she asked Rocky who remained focused on the screen of his laptop. Another cup of coffee would provide the jump start her brain cells needed.

"Her name and photo popped up on an escort Web site based in Baltimore. Looks like there hasn't been an update in more than two years. She may or may not have still been involved with that business."

After refilling her cup, Kendra moved up behind Rocky to study the screen. In the photo Ferguson was outfitted in leather and chains. If this was the other woman, did Castille's wife learn about her and flip out? Or was Grant's accusation nothing more than an attempt to draw attention away from Castille himself? At one time Kendra's relationship with Sharon Castille, the senator's wife, had been relatively close. "Maybe we should try talking to Mrs. Castille."

Rocky glanced up at her. "Is there any chance she would willingly see you?"

Kendra wandered to the foot of the bed and collapsed. She wasn't sure how much longer she could put off getting some sleep. Even a second cup of coffee wasn't doing the trick. "I suppose it depends upon how the senator explained my abrupt departure from his staff. Can't hurt to try."

"I have a plan." Rocky pushed up from the desk. He covered the two steps between them and joined her on the foot of the bed. "You need sleep."

Kendra motioned to the door. "I should call the front desk about my room."

Rocky moved his head from side to side. "You sleep." He patted the bed. "I'll do a little more research, then I'll crash out in the chair."

She couldn't do that. It would be…inappropriate. Absolutely. Inappropriate. "I'm sure they'll give me another room." Kendra stared at her lap where her clasped hands tightened in uncertainty around the cup.

"Look. I'll call the front desk about your room. Don't worry about that." He curled his forefinger beneath her chin and lifted her gaze to his. "But, for tonight, I want you where I can see you."

His touch or maybe his voice made her tremble just a little. Could have been the exhaustion. "I'll be fine." She was perfectly capable of taking care of herself. His suggestion that she couldn't was…ridiculous. She had taken care of herself during dicey field investigations before.

He dropped his hand, gave her a patient

smile. "I'm certain you would be fine either way, but I wouldn't be fine at all."

Confusion lined her brow.

"I'd spend the rest of the night worried about the possibility that whoever did that" he pointed in the direction of her room "would come back. I could conduct this investigation alone." He nodded for emphasis. "Don't think I can't. This whole partners gig is the Colby way of doing things."

She opened her mouth to argue the idea, but he kept going. "The bottom line is that I need you on this one. I don't know the players or their worlds. Your knowledge and your contacts will make what has to be done a whole lot easier and more efficient. Not to mention I know how much this case means to you. So let's not take any chances with safety. Yours or mine. You crash here and we can keep an eye on each other."

Maybe it was the genuine concern in those blue eyes of his…or maybe it was just her need to feel protected at the moment.

As much as she'd like to claim immunity to vulnerability, that would be a lie.

Determined, aggressive, she was both those things but she was also a woman and right now she felt a little vulnerable.

"I can't argue with your reasoning, partner." She exhaled the remainder of her uncertainty. "Wake me up if you find anything."

"Will do."

Rocky returned to his laptop. Kendra didn't move for a time. Instead, she watched the man whose nickname gave the impression of hard, unyielding fortitude. In the past fourteen or so hours she had learned that wasn't the case at all.

Big, tough Leland "Rocky" Rockford was soft and caring on the inside.

A smile widened her weary lips. She liked that.

She pushed up and moved to the side of the bed, kicking her shoes off as she went. Drawing the covers back, she decided that sleeping in her jacket would be counterproductive. She shouldered out of it and tossed it on the foot of the bed. Her holstered cell phone went on the bedside table.

Kendra stretched her kinked muscles, started to climb into the bed but abruptly realized that this suit was the only usable wardrobe element she had left. The jeans absolutely didn't count. Outside going shopping first thing in the morning, which was not on her agenda, she had little choice but to get under the covers and slip the skirt off as well.

With a camisole beneath the blouse, there was no reason she couldn't take that off, too. Otherwise she'd be a wrinkled mess in the morning. With a quick glance to ensure Rocky was absorbed in his work, she unbuttoned and peeled off the blouse.

Dropping back onto the pillows she pulled the covers up to her neck. It felt good to lie down. The many questions related to the case churned in her brain, but just closing her eyes was decelerating the puzzling whirlwind. Sleep dragged at her weary body, promising oblivion. She slowly let go.

Rocky would wake her if he found anything or if news came in from the agency research folks. Her lids fluttered open just enough to get one final peek at her partner…and protector.

He was no longer staring at the screen of his laptop. He was staring at her.

The image of those blue eyes drifted into darkness with her.

It was nice, she realized, not being alone.

Chapter Seven

Thursday, 6:15 a.m.

Rocky closed his laptop and turned in the chair to check on Kendra. She slept like a child—trusting and innocent. He scrubbed a hand over his face and realized he was smiling.

He liked watching her sleep.

Fortunately, he'd managed to catch a few winks himself. Around two this morning he'd moved to the more comfortable upholstered chair and stretched his legs out on the side of the bed opposite her. He'd fallen asleep watching her. Her face was the first thing he'd seen when he opened his eyes at five-thirty.

Another first for him.

Not only was she the first woman he'd been attracted to that wasn't attracted to him first, she was also the first sleeping lady he'd gotten so much pleasure simply watching.

Didn't make a lot of sense.

It just was.

Patsy T.—her name was Talley, but he liked calling her Patsy T.—had called with an update. She'd forwarded Sayar's cell phone records as well as Aleesha Ferguson's rap sheet to Rocky's e-mail.

Sayar had in fact received two calls from Mrs. Castille the day of Ferguson's death. Sayar had in the next hour made three additional calls to the senator's wife. The calls from Castille to Sayar were thirty seconds or less. Two of the three made by Sayar were similarly short, but one lasted a full three minutes. That didn't confirm Grant Roper's accusation, but it made for another lead to follow.

Aleesha Ferguson had numerous arrests for prostitution and vagrancy in Baltimore as well as the D.C. area. Her mother,

Alice Ferguson, had died of an overdose five years ago, leaving Aleesha alone and to, apparently, follow in the footsteps of her longtime profession. Alice had grown up in Arlington and moved to Baltimore after her only child was born. There was no traceable connection between Aleesha and the senator other than the photos Roper had flashed.

No traceable link between Aleesha and Sayar or Castille's wife.

Nothing.

Patsy T.'s research partner, Levi Stark, was very close to decrypting Sayar's files.

They were close to a lot of information but close wouldn't solve this case.

The only way to change that was to get this day started. He prepared a fresh pot of coffee and headed to the bathroom for a shower. Hesitating at the door, he glanced at Kendra and opted to grab his change of clothes to prevent an awkward situation after his shower in the event she awoke.

By the time he'd rushed through a shower and pulled on clean clothes, the smell of coffee had filled the room and Kendra was up with a cup in her hand.

"Good morning."

Her hair was a little mussed, the only evidence she'd just gotten out of bed. His gaze slid to the tousled linens and his gut tightened. He'd fought the urge to climb into that bed with her more than once last night. He felt relatively sure she wouldn't have appreciated that move.

"Morning." He stuffed yesterday's wardrobe into his bag and fumbled around until he found his toothbrush and paste.

"Thanks for making coffee." She sipped the hot brew. "It was great to wake up to hot caffeine."

It was great to wake up in the room with you. He pushed the forbidden thought out of his head. "Patsy T. called."

"Did she find anything useful?"

While Kendra finished her coffee, Rocky brought her up to speed on what he'd learned. She studied the phone records and the rap sheet via his laptop, coming to the same conclusion he had. They had a lot of starts but not necessarily any that would lead them to the desired end result.

"I'll take a quick shower." Kendra sat her coffee cup on the desk. "Five minutes," she promised. "Then we'll get moving."

"I'll pack up our gear."

When she'd closed herself in the tiny bathroom, he packed up his laptop and gathered the rest of the gear they would need. Communications devices and weapons. He surveyed the room, decided that was everything.

He poured himself another cup of coffee. The sound of the water running in the shower stalled the cup halfway to his mouth.

Images of her naked, the soap gliding over her skin…the water tracing that same smooth path, rinsing the soap away.

He licked his lips, imagined how hers would taste. Nice, full lips that made the cutest bow when she was lost in thought. He liked her fingers, too. Long, slender. When she was frustrated she rubbed at her forehead with her fingertips.

Why had he noticed so many little things about her in such a short time? The bigger question was, why had he been paying that much attention? Good thing she couldn't read his mind or she would likely think he was losing it or some kind of perv.

The roar of the blow dryer in the bathroom prodded Rocky from the distracting thoughts. He pulled on socks and boots. Threaded his belt through the loops of his jeans and fastened it. Then dragged on a sports jacket—his usual concession to the suit thing. A quick thread of his fingers through his hair and he was good to go.

The bathroom door opened, releasing a burst of sweet-smelling steam, and Kendra stepped out. "You were right," she said, looking and sounding well rested.

"Yeah?" His gaze immediately traced a path from her bare feet up those shapely legs to the hem of her skirt. He blinked, forced his attention to her face, which was every bit as distracting as the rest of her.

"Sleep was what I needed." She pulled on the cream-colored jacket she'd worn the day before. "I feel better prepared to move forward."

"Good." Efforts to banish the way her blouse had tightened against her breasts while she'd shouldered into the jacket proved futile. The more alone time he spent with her the less control he appeared to have.

"I'd like to go to my room." She stepped into her shoes, simultaneously stuffing something into her pocket. "See if any of my stuff survived." A search of her purse produced her keycard.

"Sure." He followed her out the door, annoyed that he'd slipped into one-word mode like a teenager suffering from lust overdose.

As she tucked her keycard into the slot on her door, he noticed that a hint of lace peeked from her jacket pocket. He blinked, swallowed. Pink lace. His attention instantly settled on the way her skirt molded to her backside. The way she dressed he'd expected plain white cotton undies…not pink lace.

The door of her room abruptly opened and Wayne Burton filled the space. "I tried your cell phone."

"What're you doing in my room?" she demanded.

Rocky had been about to voice the same question.

Burton backed up, allowing them entrance into Kendra's hotel room. "Management called in the breaking and entering. When I heard it was your room, I came right over."

Nice. A homicide detective for a B&E. Rocky was duly unimpressed.

Crime scene techs and a couple of uniformed cops were rifling through Kendra's stuff.

"I'll need a list of what's missing," Burton said to Kendra.

While Kendra briefed her *friend* on the missing items, Rocky watched his reaction. An occasional glance in Rocky's direction confirmed that Burton was doing the same thing.

Something Burton said had Kendra's

temper rising. Rocky had missed whatever was said because his attention had abruptly diverted to where the pink lace had inched its way farther out of her pocket.

Rocky moved in closer to her and frowned at Burton. "Any thoughts on how someone discovered where Kendra is staying?" he demanded of Burton as he covertly snatched the scrap of pink lace from her jacket pocket and shoved it deep into his own.

She glared at Rocky, still furious at the situation.

"Is that an accusation, Mr. Rockford?"

Rocky looked the cop straight in the eye and answered honestly, "Yes."

The stare-off lasted about five seconds before Burton's expression relaxed and he threw out a challenge of his own. "Do you have reason to believe this incident had something to do with Kendra personally versus a random act of burglary?"

"You mean a random act like Yoni Sayar's murder?" Rocky countered.

"Just do what you have to do," Kendra

snapped. Then she took a breath. "May I have whatever's left of my personal things?"

Burton backed off. "Sure."

He walked over to where her bag lay on the floor. Rocky hadn't noticed until then that the clothing items that had been spewed over the floor were now tucked back into the bag. Which meant Burton had gone through her things. Touched her stuff.

Renewed fury boiled up inside Rocky.

"Let's go." Kendra turned to him, bag in hand.

Rocky sent a final sour look in Burton's direction before executing an about-face and stalking back to the room across the hall. Inserting the keycard twice was necessary since he was too ticked off to do it right the first time.

When the door had closed behind them, Kendra flung her bag on the bed. "He's watching us." She set her hands on her hips and shook her head. "I knew it was likely but it really makes me angry to have it confirmed. Wayne is treating me like a suspect!"

Unable to stifle the assessment, Rocky opened his mouth and promptly inserted his foot. "I'm not so sure Burton keeping an eye on you has much to do with Sayar's murder case."

Kendra stopped picking through her damaged clothes and glared at him. "What does that mean?"

The taste of boot still on his tongue, Rocky shrugged. "The former personal connection between the two of you is Burton's top priority where you're concerned. At least, that's the way it looks to me."

"He told you this?" she demanded.

Rocky heaved a sighed. "No. But I'm not blind. You are," he said pointedly, "if you don't recognize his underlying motive. He's still got a thing for you."

Irritation flashing in her eyes, she swung her attention back to her stuff. "Whatever."

Yeah, whatever.

She fisted a wad of white lace and

deserted her search. “I’ll be ready in a minute.”

He watched her storm toward the bathroom door before saying, “You might want this.” She stopped and turned back to him, her free hand resting on the door. He pulled the lacy pink panties from his jacket pocket and walked over to hand the racy lingerie to her.

Her jaw went slack as she accepted the scrap of fabric. She patted her pocket, her cheeks turning as pink as the sexy panties.

Before she could demand how he’d ended up with her panties, he explained, “While you were railing at Burton, they popped out of your pocket. I grabbed them and tucked them into mine.” He shrugged when she continued to stare at him in utter outrage and humiliation. “I didn’t want you to be embarrassed in front of all those guys.” Every tech and cop in the room was male.

She didn’t say a word. She pushed into the bathroom and then slammed the door between them.

That was what he got for trying to be a gentleman.

Rocky wandered to the window and stared out at the promise of a hot, sultry day. His behavior was unacceptable. He needed to stop looking at her as a woman and start focusing more intently on the case. Difficult to do, though.

The bathroom door opened and he turned to face whatever she had to say next. He'd crossed the line to a degree and he owed her an apology.

"Look," he said before she could launch what would no doubt be a lecture about professionalism, "I apologize for making you uncomfortable. I thought I—"

"Why would you apologize?" she asked, surprising him. "You saved me from being the object of cop jokes for days. I appreciate it. Thank you."

Wow. He hadn't expected that. "Good." Back to the one-word reactions.

"Let's get going." She shouldered her purse. "We need to eat." She pressed a palm to her flat middle. "I'm starving. Then we're going to see what we can find out about Mrs. Castille. Maybe talk to her."

Rocky picked up the bag with his laptop and their other gear. "What about the press conference?"

"We already know what they're going to say. Why waste our time?"

"Agreed."

Rocky mentally kicked himself as he followed her along the corridor. Pink lace panties shouldn't lessen his IQ. He hesitated at the bank of elevators and pushed the call button. The pink lace hadn't lowered his intelligence level, the idea that she'd worn them did that all by itself.

The warning chime that a car had arrived and the opening of the doors dragged him from the troubling thoughts. When Kendra didn't move through the open doors he followed her gaze back in the direction of her room just in time to get a glimpse of Burton ducking quickly back inside.

"He's watching us," Kendra murmured.

"He's watching you," Rocky countered.

Her gaze bumped into his. "It's way more complicated than that."

Rocky couldn't ignore the worry in her eyes. "You're right. Every aspect of this investigation is complicated. Including that cop."

She held his gaze, preventing him from drawing a breath.

With every fiber of his being he wanted to kiss her. To touch those lips with his own for just a moment…one or two seconds.

The elevator doors closed behind her. He told himself to reach around her and push the call button again, but that wasn't happening.

She blinked, turned her back and pushed the call button herself.

Rocky started mentally kicking himself again.

The doors opened and they stepped into the empty car. It was early. Not much movement from the other guests yet. Rocky leaned against the back of the car and let the tension flow out of him. Kendra selected the lobby floor and took a position against that same wall, no more than fifteen or eighteen inches between them.

Soft music whispered in the air. Elevator music. He worked to focus on the tune and not the scent of soap on her skin.

“Do me a favor, Rocky.”

He braced for her censure, turned his face to hers as the elevator bumped to a stop on the lobby floor. “Name it, partner.” She was his partner in this investigation. Professional partner.

“Next time you look at me the way you did a minute ago,” she pushed away from the wall but kept her gaze fixed on his, “do something about it or walk away.”

He watched her stride out of the elevator and across the marble lobby before he had the presence of mind to follow.

Do something about it?

He could do that.

The thought had him licking his lips.

No, he couldn’t do that.

His attention lit on her once more as she waited at the main exit.

But he would.

Eventually.

It was feeling more and more inevitable.

10:40 a.m.

KENDRA LEANED FORWARD as Rocky made the turn into the private drive of the Castille estate. A limo sat in front of the stately home, the uniformed driver fitting luggage into the trunk.

"Looks like we got here just in time."

Kendra made an agreeable sound.

"No reason to expect the senator will show up?"

"According to Castille's secretary, he's in the office all morning. A lunch appointment at one, but otherwise he'll be in his office all day preparing some big presentation."

"Then the missus is going away for…" Rocky grunted as he parked behind the limo and got a closer look at the stack of designer luggage in the truck "…for a week or two."

Kendra chuckled. "Maybe for the weekend." She reached for her door. "The lady likes to travel in style with every possible accessory. A senator's wife never knows what might come up."

They rounded the hood and approached the driver together. "My name is Kendra Todd," Kendra said when the driver had finished sizing her up with a critical eye. "I'm here to see Mrs. Castille."

"Is Mrs. Castille expecting you?" a male voice behind her demanded.

Kendra's attention moved to the grand steps that fronted the house. Andrew… something, Mrs. Castille's personal assistant, descended a step or two as he waited for Kendra's response.

"Andrew, it's good to see you." Kendra used the ruse to approach the steps. "This is my friend Leland Rockford." She gestured to the man beside her. "I'm in town for a couple of days and I wanted to stop by and say hello to Mrs. Castille."

"I'm afraid she's unavailable at the moment," he said in a condescending tone.

Kendra claimed one step upward, defying his decree. "Why don't I leave my number?

That way if she has the time she can call me while I'm in town."

Andrew pulled out his PalmPilot. "I'll pass along the message."

"Eight-seven-two," Kendra began.

"Andrew, is the car ready?" Mrs. Castille appeared at the door.

"Mrs. Castille." Kendra jumped at the opening, moving up the steps despite Andrew's scathing glare. "I was just leaving my number with Andrew."

"Kendra." The senator's wife pasted on a smile. "Judd didn't tell me you were in town."

Kendra accepted a quick cheek-to-cheek hug. "He's such a busy man. I'm sure he has far more on his mind than my itinerary."

"Andrew, tell the driver I'll be a few minutes." Sharon Castille motioned for Kendra to come inside. "Let's have a coffee." She managed a more genuine smile for Rocky. "Who's your friend, dear?"

Kendra made the belated introductions as she and Rocky followed the senator's wife into her parlor. Andrew disappeared down the entry hall, probably to usher the kitchen help to prepare a tray. Or to call the senator and alert him to their presence.

"You're here on business?" Sharon asked when they'd settled amid her luxurious furnishings.

Kendra chose a fairly direct approach. "I'm here to support Yoni's family. I was devastated to hear of his death."

Hesitation. Blink. "Yes…it's just awful. The senator says he'll be greatly missed."

"I know he was a good friend to you both," Kendra suggested.

Two blinks this time. Blank expression. "I'm sorry to say I didn't know him that well. I saw him a few times at social events and occasionally at Judd's office. Still, it's tragic. Just tragic."

By the time she'd finished speaking her voice had reached that sympathetic tone she'd clearly been striving for. Too bad she'd had to work so hard to accomplish her goal.

"You saw the press conference this morning?" Another couple of rapid blinks.

"Yes." Kendra worked equally hard to restrain her anger. What was the woman hiding? Yoni was dead! Was there no one close to him who cared to see that justice was served?

"Tragic," Sharon repeated. "Just tragic."

Kendra went for broke. "Yoni mentioned to me that the two of you spoke occasionally. By phone, I believe he said."

Despite the store-bought blush applied so meticulously to her cheeks, the color drained from Sharon's face. "Really? I can't recall speaking to him by phone?" She pressed a finger to her lips, then said, "Perhaps there was that once...when Judd was out of town." She shook her head. "I'm not sure actually."

"I could be mistaken," Kendra offered, then frowned as if trying to recall the conversation. "Maybe it was someone else." She shook her head. "It was last month. I may have the whole thing confused." She feigned a laugh at her confusion. "He kept talking about some automobile accident. Doesn't matter anyway. So," Kendra stared into the woman's startled gaze, "how have you been?"

The conversation turned short and crisp from there. The coffee tray never arrived. Within ten minutes of their arrival Sharon appeared to suddenly remember that she was on her way to her sister's house in Alexandria. She really had to go. The driver was waiting after all.

Rocky guided the rental car around the circle driveway and back onto the street. "I think that's the first time I've been in a room with two other people and not said a word."

Kendra laughed, mostly because she was frustrated and disappointed and needed a break in the tension. "I assumed you were too busy analyzing the target to speak."

"It didn't require that much effort."

Kendra made another sound that couldn't quite be labeled a laugh. Rocky was definitely right about that. Sharon Castille had lied through her perfect white teeth. She was probably on the phone to the senator right now.

How was it that the people closest to Yoni could care so little for his life that they would cover up the truth about his death?

There was only one reason.

To cover up their own guilt.

"You up to a little street walking?" Rocky asked, dragging her from the painful thoughts.

Kendra turned in her seat to study his profile. "I was just thinking that should be our next move."

"Great minds and all that jazz." He shot her a smile.

She liked his smile. Liked spending time with him. She'd been alone for so long. It hadn't bothered her until now. Funny. "So," she redirected her thoughts to their next step, "that gives us a few hours."

The ladies of the night preferred the dark. "I'd like to do some research on the Transparency Bill Yoni talked about. Find out who supports it, who's against it. Maybe something will jump out at me."

"Where to?" he asked.

"The library."

"Just tell me the way."

"Take the same route back to D.C. proper that we came." That he kept checking the rearview mirror as she talked tripped an internal alarm. "Something wrong?"

"Nothing I can't handle." He made an abrupt right.

Kendra braced, keeping an eye on the side mirror for their tail.

Rocky had no more straightened out from the turn than a silver sedan skidded into the same turn.

"I hope you know this area well." Rocky stomped the accelerator.

"Fairly well." She kept her focus on the street signs. Hoped her memory didn't fail her.

"Take the next left." That would take them back to the Beltway where they could more easily get lost in the traffic.

Rocky barreled into the turn, skidding wide. Kendra held her breath. Horns blared as they crossed traffic out of turn.

They hit the Beltway, pushing well beyond the posted speed limit. A few abrupt lane changes and a last-minute exit and the silver sedan was no longer in the rearview mirror.

Rocky doubled back one exit and reentered the Beltway. He laid back with the slower traffic in the right lane.

"Good job." Kendra exhaled some of her tension.

"For now." Rocky sent her a pointed look. "Whether it was your visit with Burton or Mrs. Castille, someone's marked you for surveillance."

Which had to mean they were getting warmer.

Chapter Eight

L Street, 9:05 p.m.

Rocky wrapped his arm around Kendra's shoulders. The move startled her at first but then she recognized that it was designed to ensure they didn't stand out. She relaxed. Most of the couples were holding hands or wrapped in each other's arms as they cruised the popular street.

If anyone had tailed them to or from the library they were very good at covert surveillance. Neither Rocky nor Kendra had picked up on a tail.

Levi Stark had completed decrypting the files and sent all to Rocky's laptop. Most of the information was related to the various bills Yoni had been working prior to his death. But one had proven unsettling. It read like a transcription of a meeting or telephone conversation with only one side of the conversation recorded. According to the transcript, Senator Castille had exchanged heated words with an unknown party related to his refusal to pay a fee in exchange for silence on a subject that was never mentioned.

Possibly the conversation was connected to the blackmail threat Yoni had spoken of. But no particular bill, or subject for that matter, was mentioned. No names were revealed. Which made no sense at all. Why had someone bothered to steal the hard drive from her hotel room if it contained nothing of significance?

Kendra could only assume that, like her, the thief had assumed something important would be in the files. That not being the case, she had no answers and nothing concrete on which to move forward.

Yet, Kendra had to presume that the information carried some sort of hidden significance that, apparently, only Yoni understood.

The most disturbing aspect was that she and Rocky had been on location more than thirty hours and they knew nothing useful to the investigation.

While at the library Kendra had looked up the Ferguson accident in a number of the local papers. In each instance the vague mention was buried so deeply one had to be specifically looking for the article to locate it—if it was reported at all. The one detail she had discovered that changed her view of Ferguson's death in any manner was the name of the detective in charge of the investigation.

Wayne Burton.

Too much of a coincidence to actually be coincidental.

Music wafted from the L Street Lounge. Kendra wished her friend hadn't been murdered...that she hadn't had to come back here for *this*. She wished she were on a date having fun like other women her age. How long had it been since she'd gone out for a night on the town with a man just for the fun of it?

Too long.

Maybe she never really had. Her relationship with Wayne had felt more like a necessary accessory that everyone expected.

It hadn't felt natural or relaxed. She'd never been involved with a man who made her feel those things.

She glanced up at the man holding her close to his side. A man like this one. Handsome. Compassionate. Considerate.

He looked down at her. Made a questioning face. "I should've shaved this morning. If we run into any of your fancy friends they might mistake me for someone you picked up on this street."

Kendra laughed, the sound came from deep in her belly. "You're right, you know." She shook her head, watched the couples drifting into the lounge.

Without warning Rocky stopped moving forward, held Kendra even tighter. "Hang on." He ushered her to a lamppost where he basically wrapped the rest of his big body around her.

"What's up?" She wanted to lean her head to one side and look past him to see whatever he'd noticed, but that wouldn't be smart.

"Hear that?"

She listened, heard a gruff male voice. *You show up here again and I'm calling the cops.*

"Watch to the right," Rocky murmured.

Three young women strutted down the sidewalk away from the lounge directly behind Rocky's back.

The man, a bouncer evidently, had ordered the women out of the lounge.

Rocky pulled Kendra away from the lamppost, his long fingers curled around hers, and started after the women.

Kendra hadn't recognized any of the three but she understood what Rocky saw…ladies of the night. Super short miniskirts. Sky high heels and tight, revealing blouses.

"Stay close," he warned before releasing Kendra's hand.

Before Kendra could question his strategy, he'd hustled up behind the ladies. The women stopped walking and started flirting.

Kendra took a position at the next lamp-post. She didn't want to get too close. The ladies might not be as forthcoming with her.

One wrapped her arm around Rocky's and tiptoed to whisper something in his ear. He smiled.

Kendra's throat tightened.

Ridiculous.

Rocky was doing his job. When he pulled out his cell phone and showed the screen to each of the three, Kendra knew he was asking if they had known Aleesha Ferguson. He'd downloaded a photo of her from the data they'd gotten from the agency.

The move didn't go over well with one of the girls. She backed away from the huddle. When she whirled around, her bottled blond hair flew around her shoulders. Long skinny legs thrust one in front of the other as she stormed away from the huddle.

As she stamped past Kendra's position, Kendra made a snap decision and followed her.

Stay close rang in her ears, but Kendra ignored the warning. This woman's reaction to seeing what Kendra presumed was Ferguson's photo spoke volumes.

This direction might take them to a dead end as far a Yoni's murder investigation, but it was the only lead they had at the moment.

Kendra quickened her pace to catch up with the long strides of the other woman. When she'd moved up next to her, Kendra made another snap decision. "I've got fifty bucks. Do you have a minute?"

The woman stopped and gave her a cold once-over. "Make it a hundred and I might be able to help you."

Kendra didn't have that much cash handy. "Just three questions, okay?"

The woman's hard gaze narrowed. "What kind of questions?"

Kendra reached into her purse, careful

not to take her eyes off the woman. "Does it matter?"

She stared at the cash in Kendra's hand. "Guess not. I get all kinds," she muttered. She jerked her head toward the next building. "This way."

Glancing back to see if Rocky was still talking to the other two would only make the woman suspicious. So Kendra followed her to a narrow alley between the next two buildings.

"This'll be fine," Kendra said two steps into the dark alley. She wanted any information she could get, but she wasn't a fool. The weight of the weapon in her purse pulled heavily at her shoulder, but she had no desire to be forced to use it.

The woman leaned against the building and reached into her tiny shoulder bag.

Kendra's hand slid back inside her own as new tension rippled through her even as she recognized that it would be difficult to conceal a weapon in a bag that small.

The woman pulled out a cigarette and

lighter, lit the cigarette and after a long drag, demanded, "So ask your questions."

Kendra maintained her position square in the middle of the narrow alley. If the woman bolted it would have to be into the darkness away from the street. "I'm looking for the truth."

She laughed. "Afraid you're looking in the wrong place, lady. We don't sell the truth on this street."

"My friend showed you a photo of my sister," Kendra lied. "I want to know what happened to her."

The girl threw down her half-smoked cigarette and pushed away from the wall. "I don't need your money that bad."

"Wait." Kendra moved to the left, blocking the path she'd intended to take. "Please, help me."

The woman's glare burned through the darkness. "I can't help you."

"Three questions," Kendra reminded. She offered the money to her. "Just three."

She stared at the money. "Okay." Her gaze met Kendra's once more. " But I'm not making any promises that I'll answer all of them."

Kendra nodded. "Fair enough." Big breath. "First, and this one doesn't count, what's your name?"

One second, two, then three passed before she caved. "Delilah."

"Nice to meet you, Delilah." Kendra offered her hand. "I'm Kendra."

Delilah reluctantly accepted the handshake.

"First question, were there any witnesses to the accident?"

"What accident?"

Kendra dredged up some additional patience. "You know what accident I mean."

"Yep." Delilah lit another cigarette. Coughed. "But what you read in the papers or whatever the cops told you was wrong."

Kendra waited for her to continue. She wasn't going to waste question number two if she could help it.

"It was no accident." She looked past

Kendra then met her eyes once more. "He hit her on purpose."

"He?" Damn it. The question was out of Kendra's mouth before she could stop it. But he? According to Roper it had been Mrs. Castille.

"Yeah. A guy. Dark hair. Young. I didn't see him up close so that's all I know. But I won't forget that big fancy white car he was driving."

Delilah witnessed the accident? Kendra's heart hammered in her chest. She only had one question left for the fifty bucks. Think! "This man had some beef with Aleesha?"

Delilah shook her head. Took another draw from her cigarette. "I don't think so. I guess he could have been one of Aleesha's friends, but it was the car that I recognized."

Kendra held her breath. Prayed she would keep going. Any information she could provide might kick-start this investigation.

"That old bitch had been stalking

Aleesha for weeks." Delilah threw down her smoke and stuck out her hand. "Give me the money."

Was she referring to Sharon Castille? Kendra needed to know who Delilah was. Was Delilah a professional name? Did she live in the area? Finding her again was essential. "I might have more." She dug around in her purse. Pulled out her sunglasses and thrust them at Delilah. "Hold that for me, will you?"

Delilah huffed with impatience, but she wrapped her fingers around the sunglasses.

Three, five…Kendra had five more dollars. She added that to the fifty along with one of her business cards and offered it at the woman. "Will that get me one more answer?"

Her face puckered with annoyance, Delilah shoved the sunglasses back at her. Kendra accepted them by grabbing the very end with her thumb and forefinger.

"Depends on the question." Delilah stuffed the money into her tiny shoulder bag without counting it or noticing the business card. "Make it fast. I got stuff to do."

"Do you know the woman's name? The one who was stalking Aleesha?"

Delilah held Kendra's gaze, clearly wrestling with the decision to answer. "Castille. Sharon Castille. That senator's wife."

Kendra kept the shock off her face. She wanted to ask so many other questions… wanted to know more—needed to know more. More than anything she didn't want to let this woman go but she was out of cash and pushing the limitations of her patience already.

Hesitating as she stepped around the barrier still in her path, Delilah searched Kendra's face. "Aleesha didn't have no sister."

"You're right," Kendra admitted. "I wasn't completely honest with you but that doesn't mean I don't want to right this wrong."

"She's dead. You can't right that."

"Wait!" Kendra needed to know her last name. "Delilah what? What's your last name?"

The woman kept walking. Didn't look back.

Kendra wandered back onto the sidewalk. Even if Mrs. Castille was responsible somehow for Aleesha's murder, what did that have to do with Yoni's. Yoni had dark hair and was young but he couldn't—wouldn't—have done such a thing. Kendra absolutely refused to believe that about him. Covering up a murder was absolutely not possible.

A big body bumped into Kendra, turned her around and ushered her in the opposite direction. "Keep moving."

Even if his voice hadn't given him away before Kendra's distraction cleared, his scent would have. Rocky. "Did you learn anything?" She wanted to tell him her news but she wanted to hear his first.

"We have two tails," he said without looking at her or slowing his rushed pace.

Kendra had to focus to keep up with his long strides. "They spotted you on the corner?" She was relatively certain no one had tailed her to the alley.

"Yes, ma'am. But, as I approached your

position I noticed a guy hanging around who may or may not have been part of the tag team."

Damn.

"We parked in the other direction." Getting to the car seemed like the best strategy right now.

"That's a fact," Rocky agreed as he guided her between two clusters of pedestrians. "But we don't want to lead them to our means of escape if we can help it."

Rocky executed a right face and hustled her into a cafe. He bypassed the hostess and weaved through the tables until they reached the corridor where the restrooms were located.

"Kitchen." He pointed to the door labeled Employees Only.

She recognized his strategy now. "Wait." She dug in her heels. "I'll get a table." He was already shaking his head before she finished explaining. "You go out the back, get the car and when you're in front of the cafe text me and I'll come out."

"No way am I leaving you here."

"They're not going to approach me in front of all these people." She backed away from him. "Go."

She didn't give him a chance to argue. She moved back through the dining room and hooked up with the hostess. A table situated in a straight line and only a few feet from the door served Kendra's purposes for a hasty exodus. She spotted two men loitering outside the window, one blatantly watching her.

"A waitress will be right with you," the hostess promised.

Kendra thanked her and pretended to study the menu. The watcher's accomplice came inside and took a seat at the bar. Kendra calculated the distance between them, ten yards max.

A waitress approached Kendra's table. "Would you like to order a drink first?"

Kendra checked the street again, then pulled her credit card from her purse. "Sparkling water will be all, please." She passed the card to the waitress. "Would you swipe my card now? I'm expecting someone and I may have to leave in a hurry."

"Sure."

Keeping her cell phone in hand, Kendra checked the door from time to time, covertly scanning the street beyond the floor-to-ceiling front windows simultaneously. The only obstacle standing between her and the street was the guy outside the window. She would need a distraction for him.

What about the third guy Rocky had spotted? As the minutes ticked by Kendra worried that he'd followed and overtaken her partner. Rocky was a big, well-trained guy. He could take care of himself. And he was armed.

Then again, the other guys likely would be, as well.

The two hanging around her position wore jackets with their trousers. Most any manner of lethal weapon could be hidden under a jacket.

Her phone vibrated in her palm.

I'm turning onto your block now.

"Here you go."

Kendra smiled for the waitress as she placed the stemmed glass of sparkling water on the table, along with the check and Kendra's card.

"Thank you." Kendra quickly signed the check, providing a nice tip, and tucked the card back into her purse.

She shifted her legs, settled her purse into her lap and prepared to move as soon as she saw the rental car approach.

A car rolled up slowly. Kendra's muscles tightened in preparation for launching out of the chair and through the exit.

Silver…not black.

Not Rocky.

The tinted window on the front passenger side powered down as the silver sedan came to a stop.

Horns blared in indignation.

Kendra's mouth formed the words *Get Down!* as her brain analyzed the series of events.

She hit the floor.

The glass window exploded, showering fragments over the front of the dining room.

Screams filled the air.

Tables and chairs tumbled to the floor.

A light fixture burst and went dark.

Framed memorabilia on the wall shattered and crashed to the floor.

The blast of metal smashing into metal followed by screeching tires erupted outside.

More screams inside…shouting and crying.

Rushing footsteps.

Kendra shook off the shock. Shoved her hand into the purse she still clutched. Her fingers curled around the butt of her weapon. She came up onto her knees, the weapon leveled at the closest threat—the man who had been loitering by the window.

Gone.

She swung around, scanned the people now moving around the bar. No sign of the one who'd taken a post at the bar, either.

"Gun!" a voice shouted.

Someone tackled her from behind.

Her cheek flattened against the wood floor, pieces of glass bored into her flesh.

Her weapon was pried from her fingers.

The weight crushing into her back was a patron or an employee of the cafe…not a threat. She told herself to remain calm. Stay cool. Three more men were huddled around her. She didn't bother attempting to explain who she was and why she had a weapon.

The police would be here soon enough.

Her one concern right now was Rocky.

Where the hell was Rocky?

Chapter Nine

11:55 p.m.

Lieutenant Wayne Burton glared first at Rocky then at Kendra. "Two people are injured."

Not counting Kendra, Rocky bit back. A paramedic had treated her minor abrasions and cuts. The small bandage on her cheek had anger fisting in his gut all over again. This was unacceptable.

Yet it could have been so much worse.

He should never have allowed her to stay here alone.

The cafe dining room was wrecked. Front windows shattered. Broken chairs and tables, mostly from the panicked patrons. A bullet had left an ugly hole in the vintage mahogany bar. The mirror behind it lay in a million pieces in the prep alley behind the long bar. Whiskey and liquor bottles were shattered.

All three of the perpetrators had disappeared into the night. But not without a little something to remember Rocky by. The silver car had whipped around him as soon as he'd turned onto the street that ran in front of the cafe. When Rocky had realized what the driver intended, he'd rear-ended the bastard. He'd managed to get part of the license plate number before ramming him.

As soon as he'd ensured Kendra was okay, including pushing aside the three idiots who'd seized and manhandled her, he'd given the first cop on the scene the information about the silver car.

Kendra pushed up from the chair she'd taken after Burton had sequestered them to the cafe manager's office. "I have a question for you," she said to her old *friend*. She shifted to regain her balance. The heel of one shoe was missing. "Why are you here?"

She turned her palms upward. “There are no fatalities, thankfully. It’s a drive-by shooting so far as anyone knows. There’s no evidence I was a target any more than anyone else seated in the dining room.”

She went toe-to-toe with the cop. “So, tell me, why are you here?”

Burton glowered at her, his face red with the frustration and anger he’d readily shown in his tone since his arrival.

“Good point,” Rocky said, adding insult to injury. “Working the Sayar case makes sense. The breaking and entering at the hotel, not so much so. This,” he shook his head, “surely you have homicides to work. This is D.C. after all.”

The glower Burton had reserved thus far for Kendra shifted to Rocky. “Do you think I’m stupid?”

Loaded question. Rocky resisted the urge to say yes.

Burton’s fury swung back to the woman glaring up at him. “Do either of you think for one second that I don’t know what’s going on here?”

"You have the floor, Lieutenant," Kendra shot back. "Why don't you tell us what *you* believe is going on. Clearly you have all the insight."

"You," he growled, "are trying to turn Sayar's case into something it's not. We have no evidence of anything other than a random act of violence carried out during the execution of a robbery."

"Except the robber wasn't too bright since he forgot the MP3 player and flat-panel television in the victim's bedroom," Rocky pointed out. "And the forty bucks lying on the bedside table."

Burton's gaze sharpened. "Stay out of the Sayar case," he warned. "What happened at your hotel room and here tonight should be warning enough that you're barging into territory that…could have serious consequences. You do not want to push this."

"Is that a threat?" Kendra demanded.

Burton heaved a sigh. "That's all I can tell you for now." He hitched a thumb toward the door. "I'll have one of the officers take you to your hotel."

"Not necessary." Rocky stood. "The rental agency is bringing another car." He gave the man a nod. "But I appreciate the offer."

Burton started for the door then hesitated. "If you're smart," he said to Kendra, "first thing in the morning you'll get on that fancy jet that brought you here and go back to Chicago. Don't let the past drag you down with it, Kendra."

When he'd gone, Rocky closed the door behind him. "Your friend has a point."

Kendra closed her eyes and took a deep breath as she fought the receding adrenaline. "I understand that nothing we do will bring Yoni back, but his family deserves the truth."

There was nothing left to give them… except the truth.

Friday, 1:00 a.m.

ROCKY OPENED THE DOOR to his hotel room.

Kendra hesitated before going in. "They gave me a new room."

He shook his head. "I'm not letting you out of my sight again."

"I need clothes..." She exhaled a weary breath. "I need sleep."

"I can't help you with the kind of clothes you're accustomed to." Rocky ushered her into the room and closed the door. "But the sleep" he gestured to his bed "I can take care of."

"I'm not putting you out of your bed again." She stood her ground near the door.

Rocky crossed the room and picked up her bag with its few salvageable contents. "Your toiletries are here." He picked up his own bag and poked through it until he found a clean shirt. "This'll have to do until we can do some shopping tomorrow."

She hesitated, every thought going through her head playing out on her face. Uncertainty. Temptation. Exhaustion.

Surrender.

One uneven step disappeared behind her. "Only if you're sure you can manage some sleep, as well. We're both exhausted."

"Don't worry about me." She closed the distance between them, her steps halting with the missing shoe heel, and tugged the shirt from his hand. "I can sleep anywhere, anytime."

"Okay, partner."

Rocky watched her walk across the room. How could a woman look that good with a broken shoe heel and in a rumpled skirt and torn blouse? Her jacket had been trashed, blood on the sleeve where she'd wiped her cheek. She'd taken it off in the manager's office and hadn't bothered to pick it up when they left.

The spraying of water in the shower had him conjuring mental pictures of her releasing one button after the other on that torn blouse…allowing the silky material to slide off her shoulders. Then she would reach behind her to lower the zipper of her conservative skirt. It would fall to the floor, circling her bare feet. More of those lacy panties he hadn't expected from her would drag down her thighs.

"Knock it off, man," he muttered.

He sat down on the end of the bed and pulled off his boots, rolled off the socks and tossed them aside. His wallet, cell phone and change went on the desk. The belt was next. Unbuttoning his shirt and pulling it free of his waistband was as far as he went with removing clothes. He didn't want to make her uncomfortable.

Grabbing a pillow, he pulled the upholstered chair closer to the bed and settled in. When he closed his eyes, those tempting images of her naked in the shower invaded his brain once more.

Banishing the arousing pictures, he concentrated on relaxing each muscle. One at a time. Slowly, thoroughly. His heart rate decelerated. His breathing became deeper, slower.

He'd almost succeeded in drifting off when the bathroom door opened and the clean steam, spiced with the sweet smell of her and generic hotel soap, permeated the room, awakening his senses and resurrecting those forbidden images.

He cracked one eye open just enough to

watch her pad to the bed. His shirt fell to mid-thigh. This was the first time he'd seen that much of her legs. Gorgeous. The other eye opened. She climbed onto the bed and burrowed beneath the covers.

By the time she'd snuggled in, his heart rate had jumped back into overdrive. No use denying it. He was seriously attracted to the woman. Not just the way she looked, and her refreshing ladylike manners. This went way deeper than that. He liked the way she talked, the way she moved. Her way of thinking…her compassion.

"I thought you were asleep."

Her voice lugged him out of the lust-arousing thoughts. "Almost," he admitted. *Until you came into the room and made me sit up and take notice, mentally and physically.*

"I tried to be quiet."

He smiled. Wouldn't have mattered if she'd floated on the air…he would have felt her presence…smelled her sweet scent. "Don't worry about it."

"Why didn't you ever get married?"

If she'd asked if he'd actually been born a girl he wouldn't have been more surprised. "Busy, I guess." He wasn't about to go into the psychology of his choices. His mother had a whole book of theories on his reasoning for remaining single. Rocky felt relatively certain her analysis was part of the reason he'd recently started feeling some urgency on the subject.

"No siblings?"

"Nope."

"Hmm."

He considered the "hmm" for a moment. "What does *hmm* mean?"

"Nothing."

Yeah, right. "You think because I'm barreling toward forty that I should be or have been married?"

"No…I…yes. How long have your parents been married?"

"Forty years."

"You're a nice guy. Good job. You bought a house last year, didn't you?"

"Sure did."

"Seems like you've got the whole *nesting* thing going on."

He lifted his head and stared pointedly at her. "Have you been talking to my mother?" The remark sounded exactly like one his mother would make. Had made, recently as a matter of fact.

Kendra laughed. "I don't know your mother."

"The two of you would hit it off." In a heartbeat.

Silence lapsed around them, doing nothing at all to slow Rocky's anticipation of hearing her voice again. It soothed him… made him want to hear her crying out his name.

Far enough, pal.

"What about you?" he ventured.

"What about me?"

"You grew up in Virginia?"

"Roanoake."

"Sisters? Brothers?"

"One brother. He was killed in Iraq in 2003."

"Damn. Sorry." Rocky didn't recall

hearing about that. And it wasn't exactly something a guy forgot.

"It was a bad time for my family."

"I can only imagine." His family hadn't faced that kind of tragedy. They were damned lucky.

"My mother sends me those same vibes you get from yours."

He met her gaze again. "The marriage-grandkids thing?"

She nodded. "My brother was older than me. He'd gotten married six months before he deployed. My parents had high hopes for grandchildren. Now all that pressure is on me."

Rocky didn't hesitate to give her as good as she'd given him. "So no close encounters of the marriage kind for you, either?" 'Course she wasn't thirty yet. And she was a career woman. No reason there should have been any already.

"Only once."

Aha. He'd known it. "Your *friend* Burton?"

"We talked about it, but never quite

reached the doing something about it step."

Man. "Is he the real reason you left D.C.?" Seemed a reasonable hypothesis.

"No. I left D.C. because I couldn't work with Senator Castille any longer."

"You want to tell me about it?" If she didn't want to discuss her falling-out with the senator he understood. They didn't know each other that well beyond the work environment.

"He was into amassing power and wealth rather than representing the best for his constituents. I got to the point where I disagreed with him more than I agreed. Not a good trait in a personal aide."

"Sounds like the usual fare for politicians." The words were no sooner out of his mouth than he regretted them. Kendra's education and career had been in politics until three years ago. "For most of them, I mean."

"Reaching a position that high within the government is about power and wealth to some degree. That's true." She paused a moment. "But when that desire overrides all else, it's wrong. I called him on one particular action he'd been persuaded to take and he blackballed me. At first, I was determined to prove my case…but I realized pretty fast that I was wasting my time. It was time for me to go. I realized I wasn't cut out for that world."

"Good for you. Too many people waste a lot of time and energy butting a brick wall. It's better to turn to something more constructive."

She sat up, pushed the hair out of her eyes. "That's exactly right." She shrugged. "I couldn't change the system but there were other ways I could make a difference. That was what I really wanted to do."

"What about you and Burton? Were you already over at that point?"

Kendra pulled her knees to her chest and rested her chin there. She hadn't talked to anyone—not even her mother—about the break-up with Burton. "I couldn't stay. He couldn't go." Was that really the reason the relationship died? No. "He was too wired in to things here. Too by the book rather than by the heart. I had known for a while that we weren't a good fit."

"Wow."

Yeah. She couldn't believe she'd said the words out loud. "He's a good cop." Was that still true? Maybe, maybe not. "At least he was three years ago." Didn't seem that way now. He was ignoring valid points regarding Yoni's murder. She didn't understand that. Had someone named his price? Did he belong to that exclusive, elusive boys' club now? She hoped not.

"A lady like you shouldn't have any trouble finding someone new. What's the holdup?"

She raised her eyebrows at that one. "A lady like me? What exactly does that mean?"

Rocky closed his arms over his chest and ducked his head toward one shoulder in a half-hearted shrug. "Pretty. Smart. You know what I mean."

If only it were that easy. "I'm afraid those particular skills are vastly underrated by the male species, Mr. Rockford." She adopted a knowing look. "When was the last time you dated a woman because she met the criteria?"

The sheepish look that claimed his expression answered the question without him saying a word. He hadn't.

"I didn't think so."

"It's a defect of the species," he offered with over-the-top humility.

"Yeah. Among others."

"So you've sworn off men," he suggested.

Kendra shook her head. "No, not consciously."

"What's your dating criteria?"

"Good-natured. Considerate of others. Financially stable. Sound judgment." She couldn't be sure but it looked as if his eyes had glazed over. "All that's presuming I'm dating."

His eyes narrowed. "Are you trying to tell me you don't date?"

"Not in three years, two weeks and a couple of days." She shouldn't still remember the exact date, but she did. Down to the hour, in fact, but she wouldn't mention that part.

"Not one single date?" he pressed.

"Sheesh, Rocky, don't go out of your way to depress me."

"Seriously. Not one?"

She moved her head side to side. It was pathetic now that she confessed it out loud to another human being. "No dates. Nothing. I haven't been kissed in three years, two weeks—"

"And a couple of days," he finished for her.

"Right."

"Wow."

He used that word a lot. "I would choose a number of words to describe the condition, but wow isn't one of them."

"Just haven't met a good-natured, considerate-of-others guy who's financially stable and of good judgement, is that it?"

"Guess so." She leaned back against the pillows. "Your mother would say I have issues."

"Join the crowd," he said with a laugh. "I've been made aware of my many issues my whole life." His lips curved into a smile. "My father would tell you that life is an issue."

Rocky was right. She would hit it off with his mother. His father, too, from the sound of it.

"Thanks," she felt compelled to say.

"For?"

"Taking my mind off exploding glass and panicked screams."

He dropped his feet to the floor and stood.

Before she could guess if he'd decided a pot of coffee was in order or a bathroom break, he walked around to the side of the bed and sat down on the edge of the mattress, careful not to crowd her.

"That was my mistake." He shook his head. "I shouldn't have left you. I feel really bad about that."

This big guy never ceased to surprise her. "You did what I told you. It was my decision." She shrugged. "I lived through it. And we learned something significant."

"Castille's wife and/or an accomplice killed Aleesha Ferguson."

She'd told him what she'd learned from the girl who called herself Delilah. "And that we're on to something. Otherwise no one would care to watch or to interfere with our efforts."

He traced the small bandage on her cheek. "They're getting nervous and that makes you a target."

"Makes us both targets," she amended.

He nodded. "They don't like that we're getting so close."

Close. Yes. Too close. *This close* she could see the tiny gray specks that gave his deep blue eyes such depth and vividness. She liked his lips…the cut of his jaw and the impact of his high cheekbones. She wondered vaguely if there was Native American blood in his heritage. The blue eyes appeared even more profound framed by that coal-black hair.

"You keep looking at me that way and we're going to have a problem."

She'd made some statement to that effect on the elevator this morning. She didn't let his statement or the idea that she'd given him the same prevent her from continuing to look into his eyes. Really look. The soft admiration and respect for her that she saw there fueled the warmth his nearness had ignited.

"What kind of problem?" she prompted. Did she have to spell it out?

"The kind where I end that long dry spell of no kisses."

She moistened her lips. "I wouldn't categorize that as a problem."

He leaned closer. "In that case" he brushed his lips against hers "let's bring on the rain."

His lips settled on hers…softly…softly…a little more pressure…a little more intensity…until the heat that had been simmering inside her exploded into flames. She wrapped her arms around him and lost herself in his kiss.

His arms went around her and he leaned her into the pillows. She moaned softly. Loved the feel of his weight on her…the strength of his arms.

Her hands found their way beneath his open shirt. The feel of his warm skin lit a frenzy in her veins. Made her want to become one with all that heat searing every place his skin touched hers.

He drew his lips from hers. "Close your eyes," he murmured. "Get some sleep. I'll be right here."

Her heart launched into her throat. She wasn't ready for this incredible feeling to end…

He moved around to the other side of the bed. An argument tightened her throat. The mattress shifted. Relief slid through her as he climbed into the bed next to her. He pulled her close to his chest.

"Sleep." He pressed a kiss to her temple. "We've got a lot to figure out when dawn comes."

She relaxed into the protective heat he offered. Closed her eyes and allowed the worries and tensions of the case to drain away.

For the first time in more than three years she felt connected—really connected—to something besides work.

To someone.

Chapter Ten

7:01 a.m.

He was a United States senator. This lack of control over the situation was unacceptable.

Completely unacceptable.

His wife had gone to her sister's.

Controlling his own wife had become an impossible task. She refused to cooperate. Instead, she had run away.

At the moment her theatrics were the least of his worries.

Judd stamped to the mirror and checked his reflection. He straightened his tie and squared his shoulders. Generally Sharon picked out his tie. A small thing she'd always handled for him. This would do.

His wife had no idea the pressure of carrying the weight of his office. He'd protected her from the ugliness all these years. What had he gotten in return? She'd run away when he needed her most.

He could rely on no one, could trust no one.

He was in this alone.

At thirty he had risen to the position of state representative. By forty he was governor. He'd spent the past twenty years as a senator. That climb had been the cumulative result of complete dedication and unyielding determination.

This tragedy was not going to put a black mark on his record. The only mark to be left would be the one he accomplished with this history-making bill.

He glared at the newspaper lying on the console. Yoni Sayar's name was splashed across the front page headlines. An anonymous source had provided confirmed evidence that Sayar cavorted with terrorists. The accusation was ludicrous. Worse,

Judd's enemies would attempt to tie this nasty business to him.

This had to end.

He pulled the cell phone from his interior jacket pocket that he used for making calls he wanted kept off the record. The phone was quite handy and utterly disposable. Most important, it could not be traced to him.

He entered the number. Waited for the voice on the other end. "This is unraveling at warp speed. I don't want to hear any more about the problems you're encountering. I want to hear the solutions you've *already* put into place."

More excuses! Judd's face tightened with the fury roaring in his chest. "You do whatever necessary to stop this now…today. Are we clear?"

"Yes, sir," resounded hollowly.

Judd closed the phone.

It was true. He could depend on no one!

Except himself.

He surveyed his reflection in the mirror

once more. There was one aspect he could handle himself.

Today.

Chapter Eleven

7:50 a.m.

"I can't ask Wayne to run her prints." Kendra considered the sunglasses she had carefully plucked from her battered purse. At the time she'd improvised and gotten Delilah to hold the sunglasses, Kendra had been grasping at straws. Once the woman walked away the chances of locating her again, without a last name, phone number or address, were slim to none.

Latent fingerprints would help identify her—if she had a criminal record. Bearing in mind her profession, that was a logical conclusion.

"Seems he's on the other side," Rocky noted.

Kendra wanted to believe Wayne was the same dedicated professional he'd been when they first met, but last night had indicated otherwise. Castille likely owned him as he did so many others in positions of power.

"I can lift any prints on the glasses," Kendra said, more to herself than to her partner. "But scanning what I find and getting it into the system for a comparison is the problem."

"That's one of the things that impressed me about the Colby Agency." Rocky chuckled. "You carry your own little CSI kits."

She smiled at the man seated next to her in front of the hotel desk. "That's new this year." She bit her bottom lip, considered the difference between the Colby staff and the Equalizers team. "How did the Equalizers take care of a situation like this?" Didn't really matter. They were all on the same team now. If she were completely honest with herself, she just wanted to hear him talk. She liked the sound of his voice. Liked the way he kissed even more. Heat shimmered through her as the memories from the wee hours of the morning whispered in her mind.

A grin lifted his lips, creating enduring little creases at the corners of his eyes. Something else she liked. "Excessive force. What else?"

"Ha-ha."

"You do your *CSI* thing," he offered. "I'll take care of scanning the prints and getting them into IAFIS. Don't sweat it."

"How the hell can you do that?" The Integrated Automated Fingerprint Identification System belonged to the feds. Breaking into that system, assuming anyone could do it with nothing more than a laptop and a hotel Internet server, was a serious crime.

He leaned closer and whispered in her ear, "If I told you that would make you an accessory."

Kendra shivered at the feel of his breath against her ear. That morning had been a little awkward, but waking up in his arms had been more than worth the discomfort. He made her feel like a woman on every level. Something no one else had been able to do.

Not even Wayne.

While she'd slept, Rocky had gone through her bag of damaged clothes and dug out the only pair of jeans she'd packed. One of only two pairs that she owned. The jeans only had one slash, low enough on the leg not to be a problem. He'd laid out another pair of her lacy panties that had survived. Her cheeks warmed at the thought. Sexy lingerie was her one secret vanity.

She liked the way it felt against her skin even if no one but her ever saw it. The T-shirt sporting her alma mater had only a small rip on one shoulder. The getup looked a little odd with the only other pair of shoes she'd packed, high-heeled sandals. But it was better than a shoe with a broken heel and a bloody suit.

The shimmy of her cell phone against the wood desktop reminded her that she was supposed to be focused on the case, not on Rocky's ability to make her want things she'd thought she might never again want. She picked up the phone, read the display. Her gaze connected with Rocky's. "It's Castille."

Rocky's eyebrows lifted at the news. "I guess the wife ratted us out."

No doubt. Kendra opened the phone. "Kendra Todd."

"Have you seen the paper?"

Kendra turned the phone away from her face and whispered to Rocky. "Check to see if there's a newspaper outside the door."

He nodded and headed that way.

"You do realize," Kendra said to her former boss, "that the press conference related to Yoni's death was rubbish."

"I have complete faith in our law enforcement system, Kendra. Perhaps if you listened to their advice you wouldn't be finding your way into so much trouble. You've lost that professional edge that landed you the position on my staff. I don't understand what happened."

She touched the bandage on her cheek. Last night had been a close call—closer than she wanted to admit even now. "What do you want, Senator?"

Rocky returned to the desk with newspaper in hand.

Respected Lobbyist's Murder Reveals Ties to Terrorism

Yoni's family would be devastated all over again. This was so unfair.

"We need to talk, Kendra. *Now.*"

Frustration and anger twisted painfully in her stomach. "Isn't that what we're doing?" She wanted to shake this fool. What in God's name was he covering up? What had he gotten Yoni into? This was the threat Yoni had feared…smeared across the headlines.

"Meet me at the C & O Park, Fletcher's Boat House. Quarter of nine."

"Senator, we—"

Dead air echoed in her ear. He'd ended the call. She stared at the screen, furious all over again. Pompous fool. He had issued his order and fully expected her to obey.

"Looks like whoever was blackmailing Sayar went through with his threat." Rocky tapped the headline. "If this story has no merit, it's a damned shame to do this to a man no longer here to defend himself."

"It's lies," Kendra snapped before she

could regain her cool. "All of it." Yoni was dead, what was the blackmailer's point in this? There was nothing more to gain from Yoni Sayar.

She pushed back her chair and stood. "The senator wants to talk." So did she, she just didn't like him making all the terms. Kendra had a lot of questions. Questions the senator wasn't going to like in the least. Somehow she had to get him cornered and responding on her terms.

"I guess we have his full attention."

"That's the thing about politicians, Rocky," she explained as she grabbed her purse. "Even when you have their full attention, you never know how they're going to spin what you believe you have."

Fletcher's Boat House,
Chesapeake & Ohio Canal Park,
8:43 a.m.

FLETCHER'S, WHICH OFFERED boat rentals and concession services for this area of the park, was closed at this hour of the morning. The parking lot was empty. Rocky had scoped out a slot on the far side of the building to avoid being spotted right away.

He wasn't too keen on meeting Castille in an out-of-the-way location like this. He and Kendra had every reason to believe Castille was behind the drive-by shooting last night, if not the termination of Sayar's life. Who else had anything to gain by forcing Kendra off the search for the truth? So far, Castille was the top name on that too-short list.

This could be a trap. With that in mind, Kendra had notified the Colby Agency as to their planned movements. Unsatisfied with the openness of the location, Rocky had insisted on taking a position in the trees that flanked the parking lot. Once Castille arrived, depending upon where he parked and whether or not he approached Kendra or she approached him, Rocky would adjust his position for the best possible backup scenario.

He tightened his grip on his weapon. This time he intended to make sure Kendra stayed safe.

A black luxury sedan rolled into the

parking lot. Rocky scanned the interior of the vehicle. A driver up front and Castille in the back. No other occupants were readily visible.

He'd warned Kendra not to get out of the car. To force Castille to come to her. Rocky hoped she would heed his advice.

The car circled the lot, then parked beside the rental where Kendra waited. Castille got out before the driver could come around and open his door. Looked like the man was in a huff this morning.

"Hold your position until the driver is back in the car," Rocky ordered his partner via the communications link.

"Copy that." Kendra held her position until the driver had gotten back behind the wheel and closed the door.

Rocky watched her movements as she emerged from the rental, while monitoring Castille's, as well. As Kendra approached the man, Rocky braced for trouble.

"Whatever you think you're doing," Castille said as soon as she'd come to a stop in front of him, "you are making a monumental mistake. One that will only detract from the truth you claim to be seeking."

"What truth is that?" Kendra demanded. "Your version of the truth or the actual truth?"

"My wife has nothing to do with any of this," he roared, his tone literally vibrating with fury. "Stay away from her."

"Were you aware that last month she sustained damage to that very nice *white* car you bought her for Christmas three years ago?"

"What're you talking about?" he demanded, the fury evolving into a low growl.

Rocky watched the senator's body language very carefully. The man kept his arms at his sides. If he made a move toward the interior of his jacket, Rocky was going to make a move of his own...one that would likely land him in prison for the rest of his natural life.

"June 2," Kendra explained. "There was a hit-and-run on L Street. The victim died at the scene. I have an eyewitness who says it was your wife driving that car."

Castille's arm came up.

Rocky braced.

The senator shook his finger at Kendra. "Do not include my wife's name in your ridiculous theories! She spent a week with her sister in Alexandria the first part of last month. She wasn't even here!"

"Perhaps she was jealous of your involvement with Aleesha Ferguson," Kendra suggested, ignoring the alibi he'd tossed out. "Or maybe she just enjoys spending time with her sister rather than you."

Castille took a threatening step toward her.

Rocky leveled his weapon. Cleared his brain of all else save for a clean head shot.

"I will see that you're held responsible for spreading such lies!"

Kendra didn't flinch. "You sound almost as if you really believe that."

Rocky held his breath. She was pushing hard.

Castille suddenly executed a three-sixty, scanning the woods. "Where's your friend? I'm certain you didn't come without him."

"This is between you and me, Senator," she hedged. "A private conversation about the truth."

"Is he filming this meeting?" Castille glanced around again. "Is that your game?"

Kendra fully recognized that Castille wasn't going to let the idea of Rocky's hidden presence go. "He's here for my protection," she admitted. "There's no camera or other documentary source."

"Tell him to come out," Castille demanded. "I want him here where I can see him or I'm not saying another word."

That the senator appeared prepared to continue their conversation suggested that he in fact had something else to say. That was more than she'd hoped for. "All right." Kendra motioned for Rocky to join them. Though he'd heard the senator's demand, the goal was for Castille to believe the conversation thus far had only been between the two of them. Rocky wouldn't give his presence away without Kendra's approval.

Her partner stepped from the dense tree line and strode toward the parking lot where she and Castille faced off.

When he stopped next to her, she said to Castille, "See, no electronic devices."

Castille wasn't entirely convinced. "Put your hands up high so that I can see for myself that there are no recording devices." He glanced at Kendra, his gaze openly accusatory. "Both of you."

Kendra indulged him by raising her hands. Rocky followed suit. She hoped the senator didn't overreact when he found Rocky's weapon. That could complicate matters considerably.

Castille patted down Rocky first, then Kendra. She schooled her surprise that he didn't find the handgun she knew for a certainty Rocky was carrying.

"Put your purse," Castille said to her,

then to Rocky he added, "and your cell phones in the car."

Kendra dropped her cell into her purse and turned to do as the senator had requested.

"He can do it," Castille qualified.

She handed the purse to Rocky who did as the senator insisted.

"Are you satisfied now?" she asked the man she'd once respected and admired.

Castille held his tongue until Rocky returned to her side. "What I'm about to tell you is of an extremely sensitive nature. If you dare to leak a word of this to anyone, I will staunchly deny all of it."

"What about your driver?" Rocky countered with a nod toward the senator's car. "Is he armed? Or using any monitoring devices?"

Castille's gaze narrowed with irritation. He opened his jacket so that they could see when he removed his cell phone. He entered a speed-dial number, then said, "Take a walk." He closed the phone and slid it back into his pocket, once again ensuring his movements were fully visible.

The driver's door of the senator's car opened and his employee emerged. He closed the door and started walking toward the parking lot entrance.

Whatever Castille had to say, it was clearly startling news. Truth or not. He'd taken the cooperation thing way beyond Kendra's expectations.

"Yoni and I," he began, "have worked long and hard developing the Transparency Bill. You may have heard rumors in the media," he said to Kendra.

"I've heard some rumblings." She elected not to reveal the information Yoni had passed along to her before his death.

"As you can well imagine," Castille continued, "this is not a popular piece of proposed legislation. However, Yoni and I had orchestrated a careful plan for revealing it to the public. We both knew that once the American people were aware of what we were proposing, none of those opposed would be able to actually vote against it and save face with their constituents."

"Or salvage the next election," Kendra offered.

Castille gave an acknowledging nod of her assessment. "Strongly worded advice began around one month ago. Then the threats came."

"What sort of threats?" Rocky asked.

Castille considered Kendra's partner at length. "The ruthless kind that ends careers and damages personal relationships."

"Did you report this activity to the proper authorities?" As she had known with Yoni, she knew full well the senator's answer would be no. A long-established game of merciless tug of war.

"No." The senator's face cleared of emotion.

Renewed fury detonated deep in Kendra's chest. "With all due respect, Senator," she challenged, "how could you be so irresponsible? Your lack of action may very well have cost Yoni his life?"

"May yet," Rocky tagged on, "cost yours."

"I have my reasons."

Kendra felt confident she knew at least two of those reasons. "The story in the paper this morning about Yoni is completely false."

"Indeed."

"What do you plan to do about that?" If he said nothing she might not be able to maintain any sense of professional decorum.

"I have someone working on it as we speak."

"Wayne Burton?"

Surprise flared for the briefest of seconds before Castille banished it. "Are you referring to the homicide detective investigating Yoni's murder?"

Like he didn't know. "You know exactly who I'm talking about. He showed up at the café last night after I was shot at. I can only assume since there were no homicides involved, that he's watching me. On your orders."

Castille's guard visibly fell into place.

"I wasn't aware you'd been in an altercation? What in God's name are you talking about?"

"Three men tailed us," Rocky detailed. "One of them shot at Kendra. No one was seriously injured but it wasn't due to a lack of effort."

The senator shook his head. "I was not aware of this. I received the call around two this morning that the article in the newspaper would run despite my efforts to stop it. There were no other calls."

Rocky looked to Kendra. She hated to admit it, but she sensed that the man was telling the truth—at least about that part. Even though he mentioned her getting into trouble, that may have related to when she'd walked away from her work on his staff.

"If Burton isn't representing you," Kendra asked, "then who would he be working for? He's been on top of my every move since I arrived."

"My new enemies. Men I've worked with for two decades. There are at least three who I believe would go to any lengths to stop this piece of legislation from reaching fruition."

"Yet you're still not prepared to go to the authorities," Kendra tossed out a second time.

"You are surely aware of what would happen if I chose that path."

He was correct. She was quite aware. "All-out war."

Her assessment prompted a somber nod from him. "Make no mistake, I have an ongoing effort to catch them at their own game. However," he confessed, "proper evidence is essential to taking the appropriate steps to see that they answer for their actions."

"What about the accusation against your wife?" Kendra wasn't going to let that go until she had a better sense of the senator's involvement. She had seen the pictures. He was at the very least acquainted with Aleesha Ferguson. That was a given.

A frown lined his brow. "Since I'm unaware of any such effort, I have to assume that this is yet another strategy to discredit me."

Yoni had not mentioned the troubles related to Mrs. Castille. And the senator stuck by his story. That left Grant Roper, Kendra's replacement on the senator's staff. He was the only one spouting this other theory. That he had pictures which seemingly backed up his accusations, left Kendra with no choice but to believe that some truth was buried there.

The facts were indisputable. Aleesha Ferguson was dead. Killed by a hit-and-run driver on June 2. And her associate Delilah insisted Sharon Castille was involved, if not driving the automobile used to murder the victim. The latter was ultimately hearsay but when considered in light of the photos Roper had shown off, difficult to dismiss.

Kendra posed to the senator the same question she'd presented to Yoni. "Is there one iota of truth to any of the levied threats? Like this alleged terrorist connection to Yoni? Anything at all upon which your enemies could be building their case?"

The extended hesitation before he responded warned that Kendra and Rocky were about to be given a pivotal piece of the puzzle.

"I understand that you grew disillusioned with *things* here," Castille asserted, the effort obviously painful. "I will be the first to admit that there was a phase through which I failed to live up to the expectation of those who had graciously elected me to office." The senator's gaze grew distant. "I allowed my perspective to grow skewed. The power rather than the privilege became the goal. It was wrong and I must live with those choices for the rest of my life."

Kendra let the pause pass without saying a word. She wanted nothing she said or nothing he saw in her eyes or on her face to stop his momentum.

"But, with Yoni's encouragement and support, I reached a place where I recognized it was time to give back. This bill is my legacy to the American people. I will not allow anyone or anything to taint the effort.

"No one is without a history or mistakes. Except perhaps Yoni." Castille moved his head side to side in disgust or defeat, maybe both. "This so-called connection is related to an event in his father's youth. One that is about to be blown completely out of context and grievously out of proportion."

"And you," Kendra dared to push.

"As I said, no one is without a history." Determination solidified in the senator's gaze once more despite the uncertainty quavering in his voice. "But I will not allow ancient history to destroy my family or to derail what is best for the citizens of this great nation. That I can promise you."

"Is Aleesha Ferguson one of those mistakes?" Rocky asked.

"Yes."

Anticipation whipped through Kendra. "Then it is possible that there could be some truth to the theory that your wife was involved with her death."

"Sharon doesn't have the stomach for harming another human being, much less ending a life. She knows nothing about that tragic mistake of mine."

"Someone knows," Rocky countered. "Otherwise we wouldn't."

Another weighted pause. "I can't see how that's possible when no one knew," Castille insisted. "Absolutely no one."

"What about my replacement? Grant Roper?" Kendra ventured. "Is he aware of these threats and any basis, however flimsy?"

"Grant fully supports the bill," Castille assured her. "He would not jeopardize this opportunity. What purpose would it serve? With any notoriety I gain, he is sure to gain, as well."

And yet, he had jeopardized that opportunity. Kendra had seen the photos. "Does he know anything about your involvement with Ferguson?"

"That's not possible," Castille vowed. "No one knows. This is frivolous nonsense exhumed and redecorated by those who wish to keep intact the self-serving veil of secrecy. The Transparency Bill would lift that veil once and for all."

"This has gone far beyond frivolous nonsense, Senator," Kendra reminded. "Yoni is dead. Aleesha Ferguson is dead."

"What happens," Rocky interjected, "if you're next on that list?"

Chapter Twelve

9:30 a.m.

“What now?”

Kendra dropped her head against the seat. Castille had driven away with Rocky’s warning still echoing in the thick air.

What happens if you’re next on that list?

The morning, like the situation, was shaping up to be a hot, muggy one. Whether it was the heat or the tension, Kendra’s instincts were humming. *This*—whatever this was—was racing to a climax.

Yoni was dead. Aleesha Ferguson was dead. Mrs. Castille had gone into hiding. Grant Roper had tossed aside his loyalty to the senator. His motives so far from clear that she needed a spotlight and a magnifying glass to even attempt to decipher them.

The senator insisted three of his enemies had spearheaded an effort to kill his bill. Kendra had chosen not to mention her meeting with Roper as a precaution. If the senator was responsible for Yoni's murder—which she highly doubted—Kendra wasn't about to be responsible for anyone else being added to his hit list.

Then there was Wayne. He was up to his neck in this somehow. But how?

"I want to talk to Wayne again." Kendra wasn't sure what she hoped to accomplish, but they had to start somewhere "After that we'll track down Grant Roper again."

"How about," Rocky said as he started the engine, "we get Patsy T. to run down the relevant details about Sharon Castille's car and check with the various vehicle repair shops in the Alexandria area. It'll take some time but if Castille mowed down a pedestrian, there would have been damage to the car."

Absolutely! "That could be why she

went out of town last month, assuming she left after the second of June." Sheer conjecture. Damn it. She needed something concrete! All these theories were leading them nowhere.

Rocky pulled out his cell phone and put through the call. Kendra suffered a twinge of jealousy at his easy way of talking to Patsy. He smiled as he listened to her responses. Did he have a thing for Patsy? Then why had he kissed Kendra last night? Held her in his arms the entire night?

She closed her eyes and shook off the ridiculous thoughts. They were colleagues, partners on this case. She had no right to be jealous or anything other than thankful for his backup on this case.

He closed the phone and dropped it on the console. "Patsy's on it. She'll call us with anything she finds."

"Excellent." Kendra focused front and center. She swallowed back the foolish, foolish adolescent reaction. "I'll check in with Wayne's office. Try to find out where he is this morning."

"Meanwhile," Rocky offered as she entered Wayne's number into her cell, "I'll hit a drive-through. I don't know about you, but I'm starving."

"That'd be great." Kendra waited through a ring. "I'll have whatever you're having." Finally on the third ring the division operator picked up and recited the practiced greeting.

A half minute later Kendra closed her phone. "He's in a meeting until around ten-thirty. If he comes out before we get there she'll have him call me. We'll figure out a time and place then."

Rocky made an agreeable sound.

He stopped at a fast-food restaurant and they ate inside the car in the parking lot. Not two words passed between them. What was worse, she couldn't meet his eyes.

Once they were back on the road, the silence continued. Kendra stared at the passing landscape in an attempt to suspend the mounting awkwardness. First thing this morning she'd understood that momentary unease. But now...she hadn't anticipated having to fight it again. Had to be her. She'd never been good at interacting with the opposite sex on an intimate level.

"You want to talk about it?"

Apprehension spread through her limbs, emanating from her chest like spilled coffee. "We have a plan. What's to talk about?" Frustration twisted in her belly. Her voice held that high-pitched anxiety-ridden quality.

"We kissed. Had a moment, so to speak. It was…nice."

She moistened her lips. Nice. Definitely. "But it was out of line." Might as well put that one on the table. They were colleagues working an investigation. Allowing that kind of personal interaction was inappropriate. And, honestly, maybe he would change the subject.

"Yeah, you're right. Definitely out of line," he agreed.

"It was…nice though," she felt compelled to say.

More of that crushing silence.

So…he thought it was it was out of line.

She'd said the same, but it felt somehow worse hearing it from him. Could she glean from his statement that the *moment,* as he called it, meant nothing to him? Other than…nice?

Why did she expect a mere kiss would mean anything to a guy like Rocky? Just because she had no sex life didn't mean he had foregone his physical needs. She'd been so busy recreating her career she'd completely ignored any semblance of a social life. Now somehow she was utterly out of practice.

"This is probably going to be out of line, as well," Rocky said, breaking the mini-eternity of silence. "But I'd like to do it again sometime."

Her heart bumped against her sternum as another rush of heat flowed inside her, this one emerging from her belly button and cascading downward.

Confusion abruptly cooled the warmth his words had generated. She kept her attention straight ahead, didn't dare look at him. Was she, in his opinion, just another sexual conquest? Would getting involved with a coworker be a mistake? What if things didn't work out? That could be incredibly awkward.

If she agreed, would he think she was needy?

"We should probably give the idea lengthy consideration before making a decision." She winced. Her explanation hadn't exactly come out the way she'd intended. "I mean, there could be difficulties—"

"Agreed."

She replayed the single word over and over in her head. Tried to analyze his tone. Curt? Irritated? Matter-of-fact?

More silence.

Her cell phone vibrated. Thank God. "Kendra Todd." She was so relieved for the distraction she didn't bother checking the caller ID on the screen.

"You gave me your card."

Delilah? "Yes." Kendra held her breath, prayed this would be a viable break in the case.

"Kendra Todd? The sister Aleesha never had?"

Kendra closed her eyes and nodded. "That's me. This is Delilah, right?" Her gaze collided with Rocky's.

"I have stuff to tell you...but..."

More of that coughing Kendra had heard last night rattled across the connection. The woman needed to give up the cigarettes.

"I need money to get out of town."

"Just tell me where to meet you and how much money you need and I'll be there."

"The Smithsonian. A thousand bucks."

"Thirty minutes. I can be there in thirty minutes," Kendra assured her, not wanting to spook her or to put the meeting off any longer than absolutely necessary.

"Two thousand bucks," Delilah said quickly. "I'll be at the main entrance."

The connection ended.

"She wants to talk," Kendra said in answer to Rocky's questioning look. "And two thousand dollars." Damn it. One thousand was Kendra's daily ATM withdrawal limit. "We may have to combine our resources." Of course it would all end up on the expense report anyway.

"No problem."

He didn't look at her this time. Kendra wondered if he was ticked off by her noncommittal response to…to more of those hot, wild kisses. Her blood heated as memories bombarded her.

She needed to figure this out. Later… when they'd solved a couple of murders.

10:15 a.m.

"THAT'S HER." KENDRA DIRECTED Rocky's attention to the skinny blonde sprawled on the front steps, a cigarette dangling from her lips.

"She looks ready to hit the road," Rocky commented. A backpack sat at their target's feet. A long, thin strap looped around her neck, holding a small purse against her hip. The T-shirt, ragged jeans and flip-flops allowed her to blend in with the dozens of teens drifting in and out of one of D.C.'s most esteemed tourist attractions. Come to think of it, Kendra looked younger than usual in her jeans and tee. She looked more relaxed than she had a right to under the circumstances.

He liked her in jeans.

"She said she needed to get out of town."

Rocky snapped back to attention.

Kendra considered the woman a moment. "Guess she wasn't exaggerating."

Delilah looked up when they neared. As if suspecting someone might be watching or that they might have sold her out, she immediately surveyed the crowd. When her gaze fixed on Rocky and Kendra again her eyes were wide with worry or fear.

Kendra sat down on one side of her. Rocky leaned against the stair handrail, keeping an eye out for anyone coming too close.

"You okay?" Kendra asked her.

"No way." Delilah looked around, clearly nervous. "After that thing at the café some dude chased me for three blocks. I wouldn't have lost him at all if I hadn't run into a friend who picked me up."

Worry claimed Kendra's face. Rocky understood that she likely felt responsible.

"You have some additional information for me?" Kendra asked, her words careful.

"Aleesha said," Delilah drew in a big breath, "the senator was her ticket to a better life. He promised her big bucks. But I guess his wife didn't want to share. She and that guy killed Aleesha. I saw it. He ran into her on purpose. I saw it with my own eyes."

"Were you drinking that night?" Rocky asked without looking down. He'd spotted a guy in the crowd that had his instincts moving to a higher state of alert. "Drugs? Anything that might have altered your perception?"

"No way, man. I'm clean. I don't do any of that stuff. Aleesha got me clean."

"Where were you when the accident occurred?" Kendra asked gently.

"We was talking on the sidewalk." Delilah shrugged. "The night was done. When Aleesha crossed the street to go to her place headlights came on and that white car raced toward her like the driver had been waiting for her to show. I screamed… but Aleesha was like paralyzed or something. Then…" She closed her eyes and shook her head. "Her body just kind of flew through the air. I won't never forget that sound when she hit the street."

Rocky's jaw tightened with anger. Did the senator or his wife or both think they could get away with this? Just because Ferguson had been a hooker didn't mean she was any less than human.

"What did you do then?" Kendra prodded softly.

"I ran into the street to help her…. I was crying so hard I couldn't see. My heart felt like it was gonna explode. She wouldn't wake up. I kept shaking her. Then I got my cell phone to call 911, but the car came back." She looked from Rocky to Kendra. "They would've run over me if I hadn't got out of the way in time."

"Did you call 911?" Rocky asked.

Delilah shook her head. "I shoulda but I was afraid they'd come after me if they got a good look at me. I been keeping a low profile ever since." She dropped her head. "She was dead anyway."

Kendra's eyes met Rocky's. Until they had invaded her street Delilah had stayed under the enemy's radar. Their actions had gotten her noticed again.

"Was Senator Castille having an affair with Aleesha?" Kendra asked.

Rocky was aware Kendra was having trouble accepting that idea, but confirming one way or the other was imperative.

Delilah shrugged. "She wouldn't tell me. Said it was too dangerous. She had to keep it a big secret."

Kendra and Rocky exchanged another look.

"I need that money," Delilah said. "I gotta get outta here or they'll kill me."

Kendra placed a hand on Delilah's. "We're going to make sure you're safe. Don't worry about that."

"I just need the money."

"I know you're afraid," Kendra soothed. "We have your money. If you read my card you know we work for a private investigations agency in Chicago. We're going to take you to the airport and send you there. One of our associates will meet you at the airport and ensure you're taken care of until this is over."

"I…I don't know…"

Rocky offered his hand to the frightened woman. "Come on. You'll be safe with us."

Delilah's gaze met his, hers filled with terror. "What if they find me?"

"They won't find you," he promised. "You can trust the Colby Agency."

Delilah stood, hauled her backpack up onto her skinny shoulder. Kendra got up, wrapped her arm around Delilah's. "Have you ever been to Chicago?"

"Nope."

"You'll love it," Kendra assured her. "The Colby Agency has an amazing safe house right on the water. Anything you want to eat. Clothes. It'll be like a vacation only you don't have to pay and you get anything you need. You can keep your money for your fresh start later."

Rocky hoped that Kendra would give him a fresh start when this investigation was over. He'd crossed the line last night… scared her off.

He'd thought she had mapped that same route. Truth was, she'd just survived a harrowing experience. Maybe he'd taken advantage of her vulnerability.

And screwed up his only shot at the real thing. His mother would be all over that.

1:38 p.m.

THEY HAD GOTTEN DELILAH off to Chicago. The two-hour wait for the flight had unsettled her, but Kendra had managed to keep her calm. Delilah had spent most of that time talking about what a great friend Aleesha had been to her.

By the time Delilah had boarded the plane, Kendra felt as if she'd known Aleesha herself.

Ian Michaels, a second-in-command at the Colby Agency, would be meeting

Delilah at the airport. He would take her to the safe house and leave her in the care of another staff member.

Kendra's cell phone battery had died. She pulled the car charger from her purse and plugged it into the auxiliary port in the rental. As the phone resurrected the alert that she had two missed calls appeared. Both from Wayne.

This time she wanted some real answers. Depending upon how the conversation progressed, she might or might not tell him about her witness. At this point she would prefer to be armed with some physical evidence, as well. The smart thing to do would be to get her emotions in check before confronting him.

Rocky pulled his cell phone from the pocket of his jeans and glanced at the screen. He sent Kendra a look. "Patsy."

Kendra listened as Rocky conversed with their colleague. Again Kendra noticed that his tone sounded almost playful as he spoke to Patsy.

Why was she obsessing on his interactions

with women? He was her coworker. She loved her work, loved the agency. Getting involved with a colleague could prove a potential mistake.

It wasn't like he was the only man in the world who could kiss her that way…though she had admittedly never experienced quite that level of arousal. All these years she'd thought something was wrong with her. Shortchanged in the sex department. Inept when it came to intimacy.

Now she knew that wasn't true. This man—she dared to peek at him from the corner of her eye—had proven she was perfectly capable of raging hot desire.

"Patsy came through," he said as he closed his phone against his thigh and slid it back into his pocket. "She not only got the details on Mrs. Castille's white sedan, she found the repair shop that made some front-end repairs on the fifth of June."

Kendra's pulse skipped. "Was she able to get a copy of the invoice of repairs?"

Rocky shot her a grin. "She not only got it, she also forwarded a copy to my phone."

He passed Kendra his phone. "Check it out."

She accepted the phone, catching her breath when her fingers grazed his palm. Since he didn't glance at her she hoped that meant he hadn't heard the little gasp.

Shaking off the silly thoughts, she opened the document Patsy had forwarded. "Front-end damage," she read. "Bumper and hood mostly. New paint on both. She paid in cash. No insurance claim was filed."

Would this be enough evidence to prompt the truth from Senator Castille or his wife? Wouldn't be admissible in a court of law, but it might work as a point of coercion.

Something else tugging at her investigator's instincts was how had Grant Roper gotten those photos of Senator Castille with Aleesha Ferguson?

Was Grant Roper the man who'd run Aleesha down?

Kendra blinked. Roper could be the one leaking information from the senator's office. Was he also the one responsible for the threat to and ultimate murder of Yoni?

Anger began to crackle deep inside Kendra. If she learned that weasel had done this… she would ensure he paid.

Her cell vibrated. She checked the caller ID, then turned to Rocky. "It's Wayne."

She had a voice mail from him but she hadn't listened to it yet. Oh, well. "Kendra Todd."

"Hey, where've you been? I've called three times."

Two actually. "My phone died. I just got to my charger." That was true. The rest he didn't need to know…yet.

"I was surprised to hear that you're still in D.C."

Did he really think she would run back to Chicago just because he suggested it? Please. "I'll be here until my investigation is complete." He might as well get used to the idea.

He made a skeptical sound. "We don't have anything new on the shooting," he said, disappointment in his voice. "But I guarantee I'll find those responsible."

She wasn't holding her breath. "Thank

you." Just go for it. "I was hoping we could talk soon…today if possible. There are some things I want to hash out."

"I've been thinking we need to do that. Let me check my schedule." Rustling of papers. "How about two-thirty? Is that too soon for you?"

"That'll work." She held up two fingers, then three, and finally a zero using her thumb and forefinger for Rocky's benefit. He nodded his agreement to the time. "Your office?"

"How about I call you since I may be out of the office? You never know around here."

"I understand. So, I'll see you then."

"Is your friend coming?"

Was that jealousy she heard in his voice? No way. "I'm not sure about whether he's coming or not." Rocky sent her a look. "I'll be waiting for your call."

"Oh, one other thing."

Anticipation zinged inside of her. Was she finally going to learn something real from this guy? "What's that?"

"The paper will be retracting the story about Yoni Sayar."

Kendra waited for more. She restrained the relief that burgeoned in her throat until she'd heard the whole story.

"Apparently the reporter's source had faked the confirmation. A full retraction and apology to the family will run in tomorrow's paper."

The relief she'd been holding back rushed through her. "Thank you for telling me."

Wayne said something else but Kendra didn't catch it, the connection faltered. She reminded him she would be waiting for his call and closed her phone. Still in a bit of shock, she passed the news on to Rocky.

"That's good," he said, apparently noticing her uncertainty. "Isn't it?"

"It is...but what was the point?" Kendra knew many of the D.C. reporters. She also knew the rigid rules at the city papers. No way a story would have been allowed to run without credible confirmation unless someone very powerful had a major motive. One worth the risk of a lawsuit.

"Doubt," Rocky offered.

She turned to him. He was right. A shadow had been cast on Yoni's reputation. And no amount of retractions could undo all the damage.

But...since he was dead why bother damaging his reputation?

Back to the same question: What was the point?

Chapter Thirteen

2:20 p.m.

Rocky checked the time on his cell again. Still no call from Burton.

So they would wait.

Operating under the assumption the meeting would be held at Burton's office Kendra had directed Rocky to a parking garage close by.

He studied her profile as she spoke with Sayar's mother. A memorial service was planned for Sunday afternoon. Kendra had promised to attend.

If the investigation remained ongoing, Rocky supposed he would be attending alongside her. Beyond this case and their continued employment at the agency he wasn't sure he would be seeing her again.

Since this morning she'd taken care to avoid direct eye contact unless unavoidable. He wanted to bring up the subject again and clear the air, but the opportunity hadn't presented itself.

She dropped her cell phone into her lap and closed her eyes a moment. A smile tugged at one corner of his mouth as he visually played dot to dot with that tiny sprinkling of freckles on her nose.

Her passion for her work and her compassion for others pulled at something deep in his chest. His mother would say he'd finally taken notice of a woman who didn't fit his usual profile. And now he was captivated by all the little things he'd never before paid attention to.

Just his luck.

She opened her eyes and he asked, "The Sayars holding up okay?"

"They're hanging in there."

"How 'bout you?"

She turned her face to him but quickly

shifted her attention away, as if she'd abruptly realized that looking at him wasn't something she really wanted to do. "I'm disgusted with all the misleading information. Castille is either flat-out lying or innocent. Grant Roper isn't returning my calls."

Kendra had attempted to reach Roper twice today. Jean, Castille's secretary, hadn't seen him. He'd missed two appointments that morning and hadn't called in. Castille was in meetings and couldn't take any calls. There was no answer at the residence of Sharon Castille's sister in Alexandria.

And Burton hadn't called yet.

Meanwhile they sat in the car in a parking garage that was moderately cooler than the ninety-four degrees outside.

Waiting.

For the other shoe to drop.

When Kendra's cell phone rattled, she blew out a breath and checked the screen. "It's Roper."

"Put it on speaker," Rocky suggested. He had a bad feeling about this dirtbag.

Kendra tapped the necessary button. “Kendra Todd.”

“I have new evidence.”

This time Kendra met Rocky’s gaze. “Really? I thought maybe you’d skipped town since you hadn’t returned my calls.”

“That’s exactly what I’m planning to do.” He sounded panicked. “I have to get out of here. Castille knows I have the photos. Other than sharing this evidence with you, there’s nothing else I can do.”

“You could go to the police,” Kendra said flatly. “That’s what people generally do when they have evidence of some crime.”

“Don’t pretend you don’t know how this works,” he growled. “There are times when you can’t go to the police. This is one of those times.”

“Why are you calling me, Roper?” Kendra’s patience had frayed.

“I told you,” he barked right back, “I have evidence. Do you want it or not? If not, I’m out of here. You can figure this mess out on your own. I can’t take it anymore.”

"What kind of evidence?" Kendra asked calmly this time.

"Proof that Castille is working with Lieutenant Burton to blame everything on Yoni. And you."

"Me?" Kendra laughed, the sound dry and filled with disdain. "What could Castille possibly hope to pin on me? I haven't worked for him in three years."

"A paper trail," Roper explained, "that's all I've been privy to. They've trumped up evidence that Yoni wanted to bring down Castille. And they can tie that evidence to you. You wanted vengeance."

"Since I know no such paper trail exists," Kendra countered, "I'm not the least bit concerned about what the senator is orchestrating in regards to me."

"Burton is working with Castille, Kendra. He's manipulating e-mails you apparently sent to him since you left D.C. to make it appear as if they were sent to Yoni. Think about that. Did you ever say anything negative about the senator? Or about how angry you were?"

Kendra's face gave away her astonishment. "Where are you?"

Roper gave her the name of some park Rocky had never heard of. Kendra agreed to meet him there within half an hour.

She ended the call and recited the driving directions without looking at Rocky.

He didn't ask.

She didn't clarify Roper's statement regarding the e-mails she had sent to Burton.

Since leaving D.C.

Not that it was any of Rocky's business. It wasn't. But he'd gotten the impression that she'd walked away from her relationship with Burton without looking back.

Evidently he'd been wrong.

The twenty minutes of maneuvering in traffic and executing the necessary turns were spent in near silence. She spoke only when necessary to give him a direction. He didn't speak at all.

He was resentful of a past relationship. Ridiculous.

Mostly he was mad at himself for not handling last night better than he had.

The final few miles of road were curvy as hell. Seemed seriously out of the way for a meeting. Roper was either scared to death or planning something Rocky wasn't going to like.

The black sedan Roper had driven the night before last sat on the side of the deserted stretch of road that led deeper into the wooded park. The area was secluded and deserted. After the drive to get here, Rocky could see why the park wasn't crowded with nature lovers.

He pulled up behind the sedan. Roper appeared to be in the driver's seat.

"Stay here." Rocky removed his weapon from the console. "Let me check it out first."

Kendra arrowed him a you-must-be-kidding look. "I appreciate the offer, but no thanks." She pulled her weapon from her purse and opened her door.

"Whatever you think. You're in charge."

Her look this time warned she didn't find his remark humorous.

This was actually the first time he'd thought about the idea that she was in charge. They'd worked together so well… no power struggle.

Too bad he'd made the mistake of trying to connect outside the realm of work.

Rocky moved ahead of Kendra and approached the driver's side of the car. She headed for the passenger side. If she took that as a power play that was just too bad. He'd already failed once to protect her—wasn't happening again.

The instant he was adjacent to the driver's door, he held up a hand for Kendra not to move any closer.

Grant Roper was dead.

Rocky opened the car door and reached in to check the guy's carotid pulse, being careful of the blood. Skin was still warm but no pulse.

"Oh, my God!" Kendra yanked the passenger door open and ducked inside.

"Watch the blood," Rocky warned as he

leaned forward enough to survey the interior of the vehicle. A nine millimeter lay in Roper's lap.

Whoever had killed Roper apparently wanted it to look like a suicide. But this was no suicide. "Roper was left-handed, right?"

The bullet had exited on the right side of his head and plowed into the passenger seat. Blood and tissue had left a nasty pattern over the interior of the car.

Kendra groaned. "It's not coagulated."

Rocky looked at the hand she held up. Blood covered her fingertips. Her hand shook. Rocky's gaze bumped into hers.

She moved her head side to side, her brown eyes wide with a whirlwind of emotions. "He hasn't been dead long." She nodded jerkily. "Yes, Grant was left-handed."

"Get back in the rental car," Rocky ordered. Whoever had set this up had carefully covered all the bases.

He drew back, straightened to survey

the tree line on the opposite side of the narrow road.

Roper had spoken to Kendra less than one hour ago. Claimed to have additional evidence. He didn't drive out here to kill himself. No way. This was a murder scene. Judging by how recently the bullet had plowed through the victim's brain, his killer could still be close by.

Who else had he invited to this little get-together? Or had someone watching his movements followed him here?

Rocky's pulse rate sped up.

None of the above, he realized.

This was a setup.

He moved toward the rental car, constantly scanning for trouble. He had to get Kendra out of here.

"Rocky."

She was walking toward him. Confusion nagged at his forehead. "Get in the car," he ordered again.

She held her open cell phone up so that he could see. "He said to put down your weapon."

What the hell was she talking about?

She moistened her lips, swallowed with visible difficulty, then bent at the waist and placed her weapon on the pavement. When she straightened, she peered at him, her eyes pleading. "Put your weapon down."

"No way."

Glass cracked.

His attention swung to the car—Roper's car. The rear window was shattered.

"Please," Kendra urged, "put it down. They'll kill us both if you don't."

He bent at the knees, lowered far enough to place his weapon down as Kendra had directed. Before he straightened fully, two men, weapons drawn, stepped from the tree line. From the corner of his eye, Rocky saw a third man moving from the trees on the opposite side of the road.

Kendra's cell phone clattered to the pavement and her hands went up.

Rocky held his arms away from his side, his hands up. One man's eyes were swollen, the skin around them discolored, and his nose was taped as if he'd recently survived a brawl.

The injured guy walked up to Rocky, glowered at him then punched him in the face.

The pain shattered up the bridge of Rocky's nose. He flinched, but refused to reach up and protect his face.

"That's for breaking my nose," the guy roared.

Rocky resisted the impulse to swipe his hand across his face. He forced his lips into a smile. "You must've been the driver. You should wear your seat belt." When Rocky had rammed that silver car, the driver's face had apparently had an up-close encounter with the steering wheel.

The guy drew back his fist. Rocky braced.

"Burton's coming. Let's go."

Kendra turned her head to stare at the approaching SUV. Two seconds later her eyes confirmed what the scumbag had announced.

The vehicle rolling toward them stopped,

engine still running, and Wayne Burton emerged from the driver's side. "Get them in the car."

A weapon rammed into the back of her skull, Kendra started walking toward the vehicle. As she passed Wayne she glared at him. "You bastard."

He said nothing.

A jab of the muzzle propelled her forward a little faster. When she stopped at the rear passenger side door, the man with the gun rammed it into the back of her head a little harder and said, "Get in."

She opened the door and dropped into the seat. The door slammed, bumping her shoulders. Fury blasted in her chest. With every fiber of her being she wanted to kill Wayne Burton…to tear him apart with her own hands. For what he had obviously done to Yoni…to Aleesha Ferguson.

Rocky settled into the seat next to her. As soon as his door was shoved closed, he searched her face. "You okay?"

"No, I'm not okay." She shifted her attention to the bastards gathered in the street in front of the car.

Wayne said something to one of the men. The man strode over to Roper's open car door, pulled something from his jacket pocket and tossed whatever it was, one at a time, into the car. Photos, Kendra decided. The photos of Castille and Ferguson flashed in Kendra's head. Was this an elaborate setup to bring down Castille?

The driver's side door of the car Kendra and Rocky were in opened and the vehicle shifted as one of the men slid behind the steering wheel. Wayne called out an order to the other two, then settled into the passenger seat. "Let's go," he said to the driver, then he turned his attention to the backseat. "Well, the gang's all here now."

"What're you doing, Wayne?" Kendra demanded, disgust and rage blasting against her brain.

"Taking care of business, Kendra." He flashed her a tolerant smile. "I warned you. Gave you the opportunity to go back to Chicago. But you didn't listen." He shook his head. "You should have run away this time like you did last time."

"Do you really think you can get away with this?" She laughed at the ridiculous idea. "When did you get so stupid?"

His gaze turned lethal. "I've already gotten away with it. Or hadn't you noticed."

That confirmed her conclusions. "You killed Yoni."

Wayne didn't have to say the words, she saw the truth glittering triumphantly in his eyes.

"What about Aleesha Ferguson?" How could Kendra have not seen Wayne Burton for what he was? How had she been so blind?

"I can't take credit for that one." He laughed. "Mrs. Castille got all fired up about her husband's involvement with the woman and started harassing her. When Ferguson wouldn't back off, the old bag threatened her. Sharon Castille enlisted the help of Roper to attempt scaring off the gold digger. Things got out of control and

Ferguson ended up dead. The two called me for help." Wayne's smile broadened into a grin. "It's always useful to have a senator's wife in your pocket."

"What did any of that have to do with Yoni?" Kendra demanded.

"Nothing at the time." Wayne looked beyond Kendra to the street. Likely checking to ensure his other two minions were following.

"But an opportunity presented itself," Wayne continued, shifting his attention back to her. "If the senator wants to keep his wife out of trouble, he'll do as he's been told. Sayar was only a warning. I think the senator will pay a little more attention now."

"You didn't have to kill Yoni," Kendra said, her voice shaking with anger.

"But Yoni was trouble," Wayne countered. "He wasn't going to just shut up and move on. And Roper was getting nervous, running off his mouth about Ferguson and the senator. His suicide ties up all the loose ends. You see," Wayne shook his head,

"Roper had a thing for Sayar. But Sayar wasn't interested. Roper was scorned, killed the object of his desires and then couldn't live with it so he killed himself. Pictures of his dead idol and notes he'd written to him are scattered inside his car. Too bad."

"You're insane," Kendra said.

Wayne laughed. "I'm a genius, that's what I am. Neither of the two can cause any trouble. I'll be assigned the case and all the evidence will fall into place just the way I want it to."

"The bill," Kendra muttered. Yoni was dead because of the bill. Roper, too. Yoni's integrity wouldn't be bought. Not when threatened with lies, not for anything. Wayne had known that. She stared at her former lover in abject disgust. "Who hired you to do this? How much did you decide your integrity was worth?"

"Better to walk away a rich man," Wayne offered, "than to run with nothing."

"I ran," Kendra tossed back at him, "with my integrity intact."

Wayne stared at her for too long, making

Kendra shudder in disgust. "I guess now you're going to die with your integrity untarnished." He nodded toward Rocky. "So's your friend."

Rocky chuckled. "Make the first shot count, friend. Because, trust me, you won't get the opportunity to take another one."

The air evacuated Kendra's chest as the two men stared off, the weapon in Wayne's hand aimed directly at Rocky's face.

"Trust *me*," Wayne said, "even if you weren't going to die very shortly, she would never be yours. She doesn't trust herself enough to trust anyone else on that level." He glanced at Kendra. "She likes being alone."

Kendra wanted to slap his arrogant face but his words hit too close to home. Maybe he was right. Maybe she hadn't given herself fully to anyone. Maybe she couldn't. She stared at the gun in his hand. If Wayne had his way, it wouldn't matter anyway.

THEY DIDN'T GO FAR before the driver came to a stop. Burton got out, opened Kendra's door and ordered her out. The driver did the same, shoving his weapon in Rocky's face to ensure his cooperation.

Parked behind them at an angle just past the guardrail, half on and half off the pavement, was the rental car Rocky and Kendra had been driving, the front tires scarcely clinging to the edge of the road's shoulder. The other two thugs climbed out. The vehicle shifted precariously. Two of the men, one on either side of Rocky, pushed him toward the rental. Rocky got a good view of what lay beyond the shoulder of the road. Air...with a steep drop that ended in the trees below.

Burton ushered Kendra to the driver's side of the rental. "You must have been pretty upset when you found Roper dead," he explained. "You missed the curve and crashed into the trees below."

Rocky's escorts ushered him to the passenger side of the car, allowing an unobstructed view of the ravine below. Considering the distance, surviving the plunge wasn't impossible, but highly unlikely.

It was four against two. Sorry odds any way you looked at it. Not to mention he and Kendra were no longer armed.

"Open the door and get behind the wheel," Burton ordered Kendra.

She hesitated, stared across the car's roof at Rocky.

Rocky needed a plan, damn it!

"Maybe if you'd been able to call for help," Burton taunted, "you might have survived. But no one's going to find you until tomorrow morning. Neither of you will survive." He looked across the top of the car at Rocky. "By the way, we'll need your cell phone."

The man who had stood at Rocky's right but now stood behind him considering their proximity to the shoulder's edge jammed his weapon into Rocky's spleen. "Give me the cell phone, then open the door and get in," he growled.

Rocky glanced over his shoulder at the shorter man. "Make me."

"Putting a bullet into your head," Burton warned, "isn't part of the plan, but I'm flexible." Burton sent a lethal stare in Rocky's direction. "Now, give up the cell phone."

There was only one thing to do.

Rocky's gaze locked with Kendra's. He silently mouthed a single word.

Jump.

Chapter Fourteen

Nothing but air…falling…falling…

Bullets whizzed past her.

Something hot pierced her left shoulder.

Leaves crushed into her face.

Something hard hit her in the stomach, stopped her forward momentum, sending her into a cartwheel-like spin.

Then she was falling again.

Limbs lashed at her, slapped her face.

Reach out, she told herself, *grab on!*

The voice in her brain prompted her hands to reach…her fingers to clutch.

The too small branch slowed her fall for a split second then slipped through her fingers.

Her hip jarred against a larger branch. Pain shattered in her pelvis.

Adrenaline detonated in her brain.

Grab something!

She clutched with her hands, her arms.

Bark scraped at her forearms.

She blinked. Shook her head to clear the spinning.

Her arms tightened around the tree branch.

She wasn't falling anymore.

Voices on the road above…she couldn't see through all the branches and leaves.

Where was Rocky?

She twisted her neck, looked to the right and then the left. All she could see in any direction was leaves and branches and more leaves.

Her heart pounded. Her shoulder burned. Her body ached.

A sudden shift in the air pressure made her heart stutter.

A crash sent her flying loose from the limb she'd been hugging.

Glass exploded…metal whined.

She slammed into something hard. Flung her arms and legs frantically…scrambling for some kind of purchase.

Her face rubbed against something rough as she slid down…down…down.

She bounced on something softer.

The air whooshed out of her lungs.

The ground.

She was on the ground. Alive. And conscious.

She blinked. Where was Rocky?

She wanted to shout his name but a sound stopped her.

Voice…male.

"Get down there and find them! Make sure they're dead."

They were coming. She had to move.

Something above her snagged her attention.

Black…or dark. Metal.

Kendra tried to focus.

Tires.

The car.

The car was lodged in the trees directly above her.

She had to move.

To run!

A hand latched onto her arm.

Her head came up. A scream lodged in her throat.

"We gotta get out of here."

Rocky!

He helped her to her feet.

Pain radiated through her shoulders… her back. Her entire body.

He dragged her forward.

Her right ankle burned like fire.

Ignore the pain.

Run!

The sound of wood groaning and splitting rent the air.

A crash echoed through the trees as the car impacted the ground behind them.

Rocky darted around trees, dragging her behind him.

She tried to focus on putting one foot in front of the other. On keeping up with him.

The pain subsided, allowing her brain to concentrate on escape.

Rocky suddenly stopped. She butted into his back.

A new sound reached her ears.

Water. They'd run into the river.

What did they do now?

He ripped open the buttons of his shirt and tore it off his shoulders.

"What…" she moistened her dry lips "…what're you doing?"

He flung the shirt on the bank near the edge of the water and grabbed her hand once more. "Now we double back, going wide and keeping very, very quiet."

His left eye was swollen. His nose had been bleeding and, like her, his face and neck were scratched.

She nodded. "Okay."

He moved through the woods, going wide to the right and slowly forward.

Her heart pounded hard enough to burst out of her chest. She ducked, following his movements, beneath low lying limbs. He avoided the thickest underbrush to prevent unnecessary noise.

Voices and the sound of slogging through

the brush reverberated from their left. The enemy was a ways off but not far enough to suit Kendra.

Rocky pulled her to the far right and into a tall thicket of undergrowth. He parted the foliage and weaved his way inside, towing her along behind him.

Once they were deep into the thicket, he settled on the ground and pulled her into his lap. "Don't make a sound," he whispered in her ear.

She nodded her understanding.

His arms went around her and he opened his cell in front of her. She stared at the screen where a text message from Patsy read: help is en route.

Relief shook Kendra. He hadn't given up his cell and somehow during all this he'd summoned help. She leaned into his chest, fighting the tears.

She was stronger than this…she knew she was. But he was far stronger than her. If they survived…it would be because of him.

KENDRA COULDN'T GUESS HOW much time had passed. Rocky held her in his arms like a child. The pain radiated along every muscle in her body. She also couldn't assess her injuries. Her shoulder was still leaking blood. Rocky had checked it out. Bullet wound, but it had only cut through the skin and muscle. Nothing she wouldn't survive. Her ankle was swollen…her face burned like fire. But she wasn't having any trouble breathing.

Rocky appeared to be in better shape. No gunshot wounds. Nothing broken, he'd assured her.

The crunch of underbrush snapped her from the worries.

Someone was close.

She felt the tension in Rocky's muscles.

The whisper of leaves against fabric came nearer still. Heavy footfalls. Whoever was coming wasn't afraid of being overheard.

More voices in the distance…maybe in the direction of the river.

Didn't stop the approaching threat.

Someone was right on top of their position.

A familiar whop-whop-whop grew louder and louder.

Helicopter.

Hope swelled inside Kendra.

Had to be the help Patsy said was en route.

Thank God!

The bushes suddenly parted.

The business end of a handgun rammed into the opening.

"Too bad someone had to leave a swipe of blood on these leaves."

Wayne. He shook the bush.

Kendra's hopes withered.

"Get up!" Wayne roared.

Rocky pushed Kendra off his lap and scrambled up. "Hear that helicopter, Burton," he warned. "That's one of the last sounds you'll hear before spending the rest of your life in prison."

Kendra had to do something.

She couldn't see through the bushes.

Tried to part the limbs so she could assess the situation.

"Come out, Kendra," Wayne snarled. "I want you to watch your partner die before I kill you."

She parted the foliage and scrambled out but didn't stand. She stared up at the man she'd once cared enough about to share her body with him. His weapon was leveled at Rocky's bare chest.

Wayne laughed as he stared down at her. "You don't look so self-righteous now."

Rocky moved. Pushed the weapon upward. A shot exploded from the muzzle.

Wayne struggled to pull the weapon down low enough to get a bullet into Rocky's face.

Kendra stopped looking…stopped thinking.

She lunged at Wayne's legs. Clamped down on his shin with her teeth. Bit him as hard as she could.

He let out a howl. Tried to kick her off.

Her teeth tore into the fabric of his trousers.

He stumbled back.

She reached up, grabbed his crotch, squeezed then twisted.

He went down.

Wayne's shoe heel connected with her jaw.

Kendra let go. Rolled away from him.

Wayne was suddenly on his feet, swaying with pain. Rocky had the weapon pressed to his temple. "Maybe you won't make it to prison," Rocky snarled.

Kendra scrambled to her feet.

"Get behind me," Rocky ordered.

She didn't question his command. Obeyed without hesitation.

"Stop right there," Rocky roared.

Kendra didn't dare peek around him, but his warning told her Wayne's friends had joined the party.

"Release him and we'll all just go our separate ways," one of the goons suggested.

The helicopter was right on top of them now. Not visible through the trees but there.

Sirens wailed in the distance.

"Put your weapons down," Rocky countered. "I want you facedown on the ground, arms and legs spread."

Rocky held Wayne in front of him like a shield. His quick thinking might very well be the sole reason they survived.

"Now!" he commanded.

"Shoot him!" Wayne screamed.

Fear burst in Kendra's chest.

If she made a run for it, the other men would be distracted.

The sound of rustling foliage caused her to hesitate.

"Good friends are hard to find, Burton," Rocky taunted. "Looks like yours fall into a different category."

Kendra dared to look beyond Rocky. The three men were barreling through the woods.

The sirens were on the road just above them now.

And she and Rocky were alive.

By the grace of God, his quick thinking and all those lovely trees.

Chapter Fifteen

9:15 p.m.

Kendra leaned her head against the wall of the small office she'd been sequestered to after she'd given her statement. She hadn't been allowed to see Rocky since they'd been treated at the ER.

Statements had been taken at the scene, but then after the doctor had released them from the ER, they had been brought to police headquarters in separate vehicles.

She had been questioned for nearly an hour.

Since then, she'd been sitting in this damned office for half an hour.

Ian Michaels from the Colby Agency had

arrived. Kendra had barely gotten to speak to him when she'd been ushered away.

Ian had assured her that Rocky was fine and being questioned in another interview room.

Kendra just wanted this over.

She hadn't been allowed to contact Yoni's parents. She wanted them to know that he had been completely innocent of this entire travesty.

The door opened and she sat up straighter.

Senator Castille entered the room and closed the door behind him.

Anger and disappointment roiled inside her. He was the last person she wanted to see right now.

"Kendra." He sat down in the only other available chair besides the one behind the desk.

"What do you want?" She blinked back the tears of grief that had been building for days…since she'd heard about Yoni's murder.

Castille stared at the floor a moment as if the generic carpet held some secret.

Secrets…lies…she'd escaped this world once.

As soon as this part was over she intended to return to Chicago and never look back. Again.

"I'm sorry you were hurt by all this."

Her gaze flew to his. "All of *this* is your fault!"

He nodded. "To some degree, yes. It is."

The only good she could see coming of this was if he stepped down from the office to which he'd been entrusted.

"I want to explain how this happened."

Like she wanted to hear anything he had to say. "I'll hear it all in court." She had no choice but to return for that. Damn it!

"Sharon found out about Aleesha and she went a little crazy."

Kendra glared at him, wishing desperately that looks could kill. "You should have thought of that when you were chasing that poor girl." She shook her head with the disgust writhing inside her. “I thought you were better than that.”

He held up both hands as if to protect himself from her poisonous words. “It’s not what you think.”

Yeah, right. Every cheater said that.

“Aleesha was my daughter.”

Shock quaked through Kendra. “What?”

Castille heaved a forlorn breath. “She sought me out a few months ago. Her mother had passed away and left a note explaining who her father was. I had a one-night stand with her mother more than two decades ago.” He dropped his head. “It was foolish. Sharon had lapsed into another one of her depressions.” He shrugged. “She wanted children, but cancer had taken that opportunity away from her. I told her it didn’t matter, but as the years went by it just ate at her…taking up where the cancer had left off.”

Kendra tamped back the sympathy that attempted to rise. “Why didn’t you adopt?”

He smiled sadly. "We considered it, but Sharon just wouldn't be suited with any of the options presented. She turned away from me and to the bottle."

His wife had a drinking problem? "I never heard any rumors about a drinking problem." Didn't seem possible. Nothing about a person's life was sacred here. How had Kendra not known this?

"She was careful. Always. She reserved her disgrace for late at night at home where no one could see. Including me.

"Eventually I gave in to the loneliness." He shook his head again. "It was wrong. I know. But I am human and I had needs. But it only happened once."

"She never told you—Aleesha's mother, I mean—that she was pregnant."

"That's the strangest part. She knew I had money. But she never contacted me. I didn't know until Aleesha showed up."

"How can you be sure she was your daughter?" Kendra hated to think the worst, but desperation and greed were strong motivators.

"Anonymous DNA test. Grant took care of the details for me. There was no denying. And, there were other indications." A sad smile trembled on his lips. "She looked exactly like my mother did as a young girl. And the birthmark." He patted his chest. "Over the heart. My mother had it. Aleesha had it."

Kendra couldn't pretend the man wasn't grieving, too. Still. Grant had said...*Grant.* God, he was dead, too. "Grant told me that you'd killed Yoni. That you were having an affair with Aleesha." None of this made sense.

"Grant realized the power he had," Castille explained, "when I trusted him with the task of seeing to the DNA test. He used it to push Sharon over the edge, to extort money from her and then from me."

"Sharon wasn't the one who killed Aleesha." Kendra wasn't ready to let the senator off the hook entirely but he needed to know that.

"Your colleague, Mr. Michaels, showed me the video statement from Delilah

Brewer that your agency prepared. You don't know..." his voice cracked "...how much that means to me. Grant had Sharon convinced she had been driving the car when in fact she had been so inebriated that she barely recalls the incident."

"I don't understand why he killed Aleesha. She was a meal ticket for him."

"Aleesha threatened to go public with the whole thing. Grant wanted to continue holding it over Sharon and I, so he neutralized an unnecessary threat. He had the photos and the DNA results."

Kendra had known the guy was a sleaze. "But why Yoni? Did he find out what Grant was up to?"

"That was my fault."

"How so?" Kendra braced for more shocking revelations.

"I saw Grant and the whole situation with my wife and Aleesha's death spiraling out of control so I contacted Wayne Burton. I asked him to see what he could do to quietly put the brakes on."

She supposed that made sense.

"At first, it appeared he would be successful. He claimed he might be able to prove Grant was driving the car that struck Aleesha. If so, Grant would likely be easy to pay off. Get him out of our lives. But then things changed. About two weeks ago Burton started insisting he'd hit a stumbling block. Yoni came to me with the threats he had received. At first it didn't make sense."

Kendra's stomach knotted. "He believed the threats were connected to the Transparency Bill."

"He was right. Burton had gotten a better offer. He has given up the names of the two lobbyists in hopes of getting a lighter sentence. Bernard Capshaw is the ring leader. He's being brought in as we speak."

"Wayne killed Yoni." Kendra could scarcely believe Wayne would be that heartless.

"He killed Yoni and Grant and attempted to frighten you into leaving. When that didn't work, he was prepared to kill you and your partner. He wanted nothing to get in the way of his big payoff."

Kendra couldn't believe she'd once cared about the man. It was…astonishing to learn that he was capable of such evil.

Castille stood. "I'm going to resign my office before this turns into yet another sideshow."

Kendra looked up at him, saw the defeat and the sadness. She'd thought the worst of him and he hadn't deserved it…at least not all of it.

"But," he qualified, "not until I see that this bill is passed. I owe that to Yoni."

A traitorous tear escaped Kendra's firm hold. "He would be proud."

The senator nodded, then started for the door. "One piece of advice, Kendra."

Until a few moments ago she wouldn't have wanted to hear any advice this man had to give. But, like he said, he was only human. Circumstances had prompted wrong decisions from him, as it did from all mere humans.

"Don't devote all you have to your career.

If you do, you'll end up old, tired and alone." He heaved a sigh. "Like me."

The door closed, leaving Kendra alone once more.

The memory of how it felt to have Rocky's arms around her, of his hot kisses made her tremble…made more of those damned tears slide down her cheeks.

Castille was right.

Maybe even Wayne had been a little bit right about her.

But she wasn't too stubborn to acknowledge her weaknesses and to institute change.

"ALL RIGHT, MR. ROCKFORD," the police captain announced, "you're free to go."

Rocky nodded and turned to the door. Lucky for him one of the rescue personnel had given him a T-shirt since he'd tossed his shirt into the river in an attempt to throw off the bastards chasing them. Right now, he was tired as hell and he ached all over. Bruised ribs and lots of abrasions were about all he'd gotten in the fall, except for the sore muscles. Of course that didn't take into account the black eye and split lip that he'd gotten from one of Burton's dirtbags.

He would live.

More important, Kendra was okay.

He stepped out into the corridor fully expecting to see Ian Michaels waiting for him, but Michaels appeared to be in deep conversation with the chief of police at the other end of the hall.

Right now, Rocky just wanted to find Kendra.

As if luck was on his side for once, a door opened and she stepped out into the long gray corridor.

She smiled.

He smiled back, then winced at the burn in his lip.

"You were wrong about Yoni, you know," she said. "You have to wear a suit to work every day for a week."

"I've always been a man of my word," he relented. At the moment he would have done anything she asked. He was just glad she was okay.

She walked straight up to him then. Despite all the scratches and bruises she looked amazing. "I gave lengthy consideration to your offer."

Confusion furrowed his brow making his head hurt. What the hell was she talking about?

"I decided that I don't want to wait or to weigh the consequences or anything else." She threw her arms around his neck, went up on tiptoe and kissed him.

Then he understood.

Kendra was ready to give them a chance. To take the risk.

He drew back, smiled at her even though it hurt like hell. "You won't regret it."

She kissed his bruised jaw. "I know. You're my partner, you would never let me down."

The Colby Agency, Monday, July 10, 5:15 p.m.

"DO YOU HAVE A MINUTE?"

Victoria Colby-Camp looked up from her desk and smiled at her son. "Absolutely."

He swaggered into the room. Such self-confidence. Incredibly handsome just like his father. And full of compassion for others. There wasn't a day that went by that she didn't feel immensely grateful for having him here…where he belonged.

"I was thinking," he said as he settled into a chair, "that we should celebrate."

"What's the occasion?" Tasha, Jim's wife, was due any day, but she felt relatively certain that if he'd gotten a call about that he would already be en route to the hospital. A man didn't get the chance to welcome his son into the world every day. Last week's false alarm had heightened the already merciless tension.

"Considering this latest case and the amazing way our teams have merged, I think it's time to celebrate that success. The Colby Agency and the Equalizers are now one. We have full velocity."

Victoria agreed. Kendra and Rocky were back home, but taking a few badly needed days off. A smile tickled her lips. Rumor was that the two had formed more than a professional bond in the past week.

"I think that's an amazing idea," Victoria agreed. "You call Tasha and I'll call Lucas."

Jim braced to stand. "Excellent."

The phone on Victoria's desk rang. Mildred, her assistant, had already gone for the day so Victoria took the call herself.

"Victoria, is my husband in your office?"

Tasha. She sounded a little out of breath. Victoria bit her lips together…this could be the call. "Certainly, he's right here." Victoria reached the phone across the desk. "It's Tasha."

"Put it on speaker," he said, grinning, "and we'll tell her about tonight's celebration."

Victoria did as Jim requested though she had a feeling there would be a different kind of celebration tonight. "Tasha, you're on speaker. Jim is right here."

"You'd better come home. Now," Tasha

said, her voice rising as she spoke. "This boy is ready! For real this time!"

Jim jumped to his feet, his eyes wide with anticipation and maybe a little uneasiness. "On the way!" Jim backed toward the door. "Sorry…about tonight."

Victoria grinned. "Go! Lucas and I will pick up Jamie and be right behind you."

Jim Colby bounded out of the office. Victoria blinked back the tears building in her eyes. She had already been blessed with a beautiful granddaughter, Jamie, now she would have a grandson.

She stood, grabbed her cell phone to put through a call to Lucas.

A new Colby was about to be born.

The name would live on…and so would the agency.

* * * * *